P9-CLS-990

AFTER DARK

AFTER DARK

James Leck

KCP FICTION

For Heather, Zoe and Isaac, who light the way through the dark.
And for The Fellas, who've watched way too many horror movies with me.

KCP Fiction is an imprint of Kids Can Press

Kids Can Press acknowledges the financial support of the Government of Ontario, through the Ontario Media Development Corporation's Ontario Book Initiative; the Ontario Arts Council; the Canada Council for the Arts; and the Government of Canada, through the CBF, for our publishing activity.

Published in Canada by
Kids Can Press Ltd.
25 Dockside Drive
Toronto, ON M5A 0B5

Published in the U.S. by
Kids Can Press Ltd.
2250 Military Road
Tonawanda, NY 14150

www.kidscanpress.com

Edited by Yasemin Uçar
Designed by Marie Bartholomew

This book is smyth sewn casebound.
Manufactured in Malaysia in 3/2015 by Tien Wah Press (Pte.) Ltd.

CM 15 0 9 8 7 6 5 4 3 2 1

Library and Archives Canada Cataloguing in Publication

Leck, James, author
After dark / written by James Leck.

ISBN 978-1-77138-110-9 (bound)

I. Title.
PS8623.E397A65 2015 jC813'.6 C2014-904583-2

Kids Can Press is a Corus™ Entertainment company

"There are worse things to be than a chicken."

~ Col. Stephen H. Sanders

Friday, 6:58 a.m.

I was sweating. I was sweating profusely. My forehead was glistening. Rivers were running down my back. Even my knees were sweating. The room was dark except for a high-powered lamp that illuminated the patient lying in front of me. Bryce Wagner was sitting off to the side, his face in the shadows. Richard O'Rourke was sitting on the other side of the table. Behind him, in the darkness of the room, the crowd was watching.

"Are you just going to sit there and sweat, Harker?" Wagner asked, leaning into the light. His pasty skin was dry. He wasn't sweating at all.

I wiped my forehead with the back of my hand and looked down at the patient. Strange things were happening at the edge of my vision. The air was shimmering. I'd been awake for too long.

"Slow and steady," O'Rourke said, angling the lamp a little. I leaned over the patient until my nose was only two inches from the chest cavity.

"Slow and steady," O'Rourke repeated.

I lowered my hand toward the opening and eased the tweezers into the patient. When I was sure that I had a firm grip on the heart, I took a deep breath and began the extraction. A drop of sweat slipped down my left temple. A hush fell over the room. The patient's heart was more than halfway out when the door flew open and the lights came on.

"What is going on in here?"

My hand twitched, an electronic buzzer sounded and the patient's red nose lit up. The operation was a failure.

I let go of the heart, threw the tweezers down and fell back in my chair.

Stanley Peck was standing in the doorway with his finger still on the light switch. Peck is the senior monitor of Weaver Hall dormitory, one of three dormitories at Choke Academy — where I live for 272 days of the year.

"What is going on in here?" he repeated. Even though it was only 7:02 in the morning, Peck was already wearing his school uniform and his blond hair was parted perfectly, not a single strand out of place.

O'Rourke leaped out of his chair and marched over to Peck. O'Rourke was a wreck. He'd been awake for almost three days. His hair, which was usually slicked back with some kind of gel straight out of the 1950s, was hanging down in his eyes, and his skin was a pale shade of green.

"Get out, Peck!" he roared. "These are private quarters!"

"Not for me, they're not," Peck said, glaring at me, "and Harker's in violation of Rule 1.4 of the Choke Academy Student Handbook, which clearly states that students are not permitted to have guests in their rooms between the hours of 9:00 p.m. and 9:00 a.m."

"You've just disrupted a very important operation!" O'Rourke screamed. "This patient is going to have to live with a broken heart for the rest of the summer thanks to you!"

"That's a game," Peck said, "and your patient has a lightbulb for a nose. Plus, you've been gambling!" he added, pointing at a pile of cash sitting on the coffee table in front of me. "That's going to get you all expelled."

The crowd, which was made up of six other sleep-deprived sweat-hogs from the Weaver Hall dorm, slunk back into a corner of the room.

"The cash is mine, Stanley," Wagner said, scooping up the money. "I was just airing it out."

"Not so fast, Wagbag," I said, grabbing his wrist. Not the smartest move. Bryce Wagner was more than a few inches over six feet tall and spent most of his time sipping protein shakes and getting ripped in the school gym.

"You blew it, Sweaty," he grumbled. "The money's mine."

"Speaking of sweaty," I said, "why are you so dry? Is it a disease, or are you actually some kind of huge plastic toy?"

"That does it!" Wagner yelled, leaping over the table and plowing into me.

I tipped over backward in my chair and came down with a crunch. I had a sinking feeling that crunch was the sound of my phone being crushed.

Wagner attempted to tie me into a pretzel while the rest of the crowd made a break for the door. He was just about to dislocate my left arm when O'Rourke threw himself across the room and they both went crashing into the corner. I scrambled up and jumped onto Wagner's back before he could pound O'Rourke into a pile of dust. While Wagner twirled around the room, slamming me into every wall, Peck stood by the door, blowing his orange panic whistle. Eventually Mr. Blatz, our math teacher and Weaver Hall faculty advisor, arrived and dragged us all across campus to Headmaster Sterling's office. On our way, I picked the remnants of my phone out of my pocket and tossed them in the trash.

Friday, 8:00 a.m.

Sterling is a short man with a thick red mustache and hair that floats in wisps above his head. When he arrived, he was wearing a navy blue suit and chomping on the end of a pipe that wasn't lit.

"Please fix your tie, Mr. Harker," he said, sitting down behind an enormous desk.

I looked down. My shirt was hanging out, I had grass stains on both elbows, there was a long tear in one of the knees of my pants, and I couldn't remember where I'd left my blazer. I figured the least I could do was straighten my tie.

"Mr. Peck, could you explain why I'm sitting here, at eight in the morning, instead of eating my breakfast?"

"Well, sir," Peck said, standing at attention, "I was doing an early-morning floor inspection when I heard voices in Charlie Harker's room. This was in direct violation of Rule 1.4 of the student handbook, so I investigated. When I entered Mr. Harker's room, I discovered that a number of students had gathered in order to play a game called Operation and that they were gambling on the results — an offense which could, and really should, result in their immediate expulsion. I made them aware of this, and that is approximately when a fight broke out. Luckily I was able to round them up, with a little help from Mr. Blatz, and bring them to see you, sir."

Sterling sighed. "Thank you, Stanley," he muttered, shuffling a few papers on his desk. "It's admirable of you to be so vigilant on the last day of the school year, and your final day as a senior monitor."

"I take my job very seriously, sir," Peck said, standing up even straighter.

Sterling frowned and turned to Bryce. "I'm surprised to see you here, Mr. Wagner. What do you have to say for yourself?"

"I apologize, sir, but Harker and his friends were being rather rowdy and woke me up. I went to his room to ask them to be quiet, and that's when Stanley arrived."

Wagner's story wasn't true — it wasn't even close to true. Wagner, like everyone else in Weaver Hall (except for Peck), had been participating in an annual tradition known as the Weaver Hall Olympiad. This elite competition takes place on our last night at Choke every year and includes such events as the mattress toss, the mud puddle jump and a full-contact, 1500-meter tricycle race. We had just been finishing off the festivities with a high-stakes game of Operation when Peck burst in.

"I see," Sterling said, chewing on the end of his pipe. "What about you, Mr. Harker? What do you have to say for yourself?"

"Mr. Sterling, Bryce Wagner is suffering from a terrible skin disease that doesn't allow him to sweat. I think he should see the school nurse immediately."

"Do you see!" Wagner yelled, flexing the rather large muscles in his thick neck. "Do you see the insolence! He's not Choke material, sir!"

Sterling closed his eyes and took a deep breath. "It's not up to you to decide who's Choke material, Mr. Wagner.

However, Mr. Harker, I must admit I am beginning to wonder ..." he said, picking up a folder from his desk and opening it.

"October twelfth, you bungee jumped from the roof of your dormitory, ripping your pants off in the process."

"The cord didn't break, though," I said. "My pants getting ripped off was unfortunate, but nobody was injured — not physically anyway."

"November third, you were found glued to the ceiling of your room."

"Sir, if I may," O'Rourke said, raising his hand. "Technically that wasn't glue — it was an experimental foam I'd borrowed from my father. Mr. Harker was simply my test subject."

Sterling frowned. "December tenth, you and Mr. O'Rourke dressed up as a bull and sold rides for one dollar in the gymnasium."

"All of that money went to charity," I said.

"That's not the point!" Sterling yelled. "You're not to be dressing up like animals or gluing yourself to ceilings or doing any of the other cockamamie things you've done this year! Furthermore, in addition to these shenanigans, you've had twenty-seven uniform violations, forty-three late arrivals to class, and your marks, quite frankly, are a disaster."

"I'm not sure I'd describe my marks as a disaster," I said. "A calamity maybe, but not a disaster."

"They are a disaster, Mr. Harker. In fact, unless you did extremely well on your exams, I wouldn't be surprised to find out you have to repeat the tenth grade."

Out of the corner of my eye, I could see that Wagner and Peck were both smiling.

"I turned it around during final exams, sir. In fact, I pretty much cut out sleep altogether for the past week, just so I could cram for exams."

"Are you telling me that you haven't slept for a week?" Sterling asked.

"I may have squeezed in a few hours here and there."

"You need to start taking things more seriously, Mr. Harker. Far more seriously!"

"Yes, sir, Mr. Sterling," I said. "I'll put it at the top of my to-do list."

"Life is not a joke!" Sterling said, pointing his pipe at me. "And may I remind you, young man, that you must be cleared out of your quarters by ten o'clock this morning. Mr. Peck will conduct a thorough inspection. You are not permitted to leave until he approves the condition of your room."

"I'll make sure that it's spotless, sir," Peck said.

"I'm sure you will," Sterling replied. "As for the shenanigans this morning, you'll all be serving a five-day in-school suspension when you return in September."

"You're not serious?" Wagner said. "I was only asking them to be quiet."

"You disturbed the peace of this institution, Mr. Wagner. Consider yourself lucky."

"My father will hear about this," Wagner said and stormed out, slamming the door behind him.

"Are you sure you don't want to reconsider, Mr. Sterling?" I asked. "It's the last day of school, after all."

"Get out," Sterling said, pointing at the door with his pipe.

"Have a wonderful summer, sir," Peck said, and we all headed for the door.

"I don't suppose I could pay you to forget about this?" I said before stepping outside.

"OUT!" Sterling roared.

Friday, 8:22 a.m.

My room looked like a stakeout gone bad and smelled like old gym socks. A half-dozen pizza boxes were stacked haphazardly in the corner, a small mound of dirty clothes was sitting on the end of my bed and soda cans littered every table. The game of Operation we'd been using was squashed on the floor, and there were dents in two of the walls. To top it all off, the money Wagner had tried to take was scattered all over the floor.

"Don't worry about the room," O'Rourke said, stepping inside. "I'll take care of it."

There was a time when I might have doubted O'Rourke, but that time was long gone. Anyone who could get us off-campus passes every weekend since Thanksgiving, talk our PE teacher into starting a Ping-Pong team to fulfill our extracurricular athletics requirement and make sure we didn't have to participate in the annual Choke Academy Ballroom Dancing Competition during the Spring Fling deserved respect. I asked him once how he did it. He mumbled something about his dad owning a private security company and told me not to ask any more questions.

"I owe you one."

"You owe me a lot more than one, Harker," he said.

"At least keep the money," I said, nodding at the cash that was scattered all over the floor.

"I'll leave it for the cleaners," he said. "You need to go, before Peck gets here."

"I'm already gone," I said, pulling my green duffel bag out from under my bed, wiping off the dust and stuffing the few pieces of dirty clothes I owned into it. On the way to the door, I grabbed my tablet and laptop off my desk, threw them into the bag and zipped it shut.

"What about your blazer?" O'Rourke said.

"I don't know where it is," I said. "If you see it, could you grab it for me? I'll get it from you in September."

"Fine," he said, taking out his phone. "Now get out of here, and make sure Peck doesn't see you!"

"Adios amigo," I said, opening the door a crack. The hallway was empty. "And try to relax a little this summer, O'Rourke. Life is short."

"I'll try, but I'm spending most of it holed up in a bunker at some undisclosed location in the Middle East with my dad. I'll send you some pictures."

"Can't wait," I said and slipped into the hallway. Peck was nowhere in sight.

I made a break for the stairs and booted it down to the lobby. I was fantasizing about curling up under a bush outside and grabbing a quick nap before my mom arrived to pick me up. Unfortunately, when I stepped into the lobby, she was already standing by the door.

She looked about the same as she had for the past

fifteen years of my life — shoulder-length blond hair held back with a pair of expensive sunglasses, blue eyes, lean, holding a Grande cup of something. Usually she'd be wearing something stylish and expensive, but today she was wearing sneakers, jeans and a black T-shirt with a big red butterfly splashed across the front.

"Charlie," she said, walking over to me, "you look terrible."

"They're working me too hard."

"I doubt it," she said, giving me a hug. "And you need a shower. You stink."

"Don't hold back, Mom."

"Enough chitchat," she said, grabbing my bag and heading for the door. "Let's move."

"I can carry my own bag," I said, following behind her.

"I know," she said, stepping outside, "but I haven't been to kickboxing or yoga in weeks, and these arms are getting flabby. Plus, you dillydally, and I want to make it back to Rolling Hills by six. I've got a million things to do."

"Whoa, whoa, whoa — hold the presses," I said. "Do you mean we're actually spending the summer in Rolling Hills? I thought that was more like a hypothetical situation. Kind of like, maybe we'll spend the summer in some out-of-the-way hick town, but we'll probably go to Hawaii instead."

"It's not hypothetical," she said, marching down the front walk and into the parking lot. "And it's not a hick town, Charlie. Rolling Hills happens to be a popular getaway for some very influential families. Your great-grandfather built the inn as a place he could take business partners. A lot of the people he brought there were powerful — and they liked it so much they built their own summer homes."

"So it's filled with rich, old people? Sounds like a barrel of monkeys."

"There are 1251 people happily living in Rolling Hills year-round, Charlie, and they're not all old. Plus, when the tourists start to arrive in July, there are bound to be a few teenagers. Who knows, you might even have a little fun."

"I could have fun lying on a beach in Hawaii, sipping coconut water straight out of the shell."

"I'll buy you some coconuts at the grocery store," she said. "We'll be too busy finishing up the renovations to worry about coconuts anyway. We've only got about a month before the first guests arrive."

"When you say that we'll be busy renovating the inn, you don't actually mean that we'll be renovating the inn, right? You mean that we'll be present during the renovations but enjoying ice-cold glasses of lemonade and lounging by the nearest pool, correct?"

"No, Charlie, we'll be renovating the inn," she said. "I've hired some help, but we'll be getting our hands dirty, too."

"I'm more of an ideas man than a worker bee, Ma. Plus, I've got *sleep in* right at the top of my to-do list. I've had a pretty tough semester at Choke."

"It will give us a chance to catch up. I haven't seen you since Christmas."

"We could catch up on a beach in Maui, too, you know," I said, keeping my eyes peeled for her black Jag. It was the perfect napping car: soft leather seats, smooth ride, the calming hum of the engine. My eyes were getting heavy just thinking about it. But Mom stopped in front of a massive black pickup truck.

"How do you like the new ride?" she asked. "It's a Dodge Ram 1500, with 390 horsepower and a V8 Hemi engine."

"Do you even know what that means?"

"Some of it," she said, climbing inside.

"I thought you were an environmentalist," I said, getting in, too.

"This will be better for the work we have to do," she said. "I'll trade it in for an electric car and plant a few trees when we're done. Will that make you feel better?"

"It doesn't matter to me," I said, getting into the front passenger seat. "You're the one who's always worrying about the melting ice caps. I always figured we had enough money to survive a flood. I mean, don't they have secret bunkers for people like us?"

"You wish," a voice said from the backseat.

It was my twin sister, Lilith. Her shoes were beside her on the seat, and she was sitting with her legs folded up like a Zen master, and her eyes closed. Technically we're twins, in that she was born two minutes and thirty-seven seconds after me, but that's as far as it goes. Lilith is short, lean and wiry, with blond hair and blue eyes like Mom. I'm at least half a foot taller than her, with brown eyes and brown hair that's just curly enough to look messy all the time. People used to say it was adorable, but that stopped when I hit nine or ten. Also, Lilith has an uncanny knack for keeping her clothes looking spotless and crisp. Even on the last day of school, her uniform — a green and black tartan skirt, dark green knee-high socks and a white short-sleeve shirt — looked brand-new.

"People with money don't have to wish for things, Lilith," I said.

"When money ceases to have meaning, I will be prepared," she said, opening her eyes. "Will you, Charlie?"

"Probably not," I said, leaning the seat back and closing my eyes.

"You should reconsider your motivations in life," she said.

"My motivation right now is to get some sleep, so go back to meditating about puppies or boys or whatever it is you think about."

"I *don't* think when I meditate, Charlie — that's the point. You'd know that if you'd bothered to read any of Dad's books."

"I don't think *Dad* read all of his books, Lilith. You know the last two were written by other people, right?"

Lilith's arm lashed out like an angry cobra. Her fingers clasped on to my shoulder and pinched down on a nerve, which sent an incredible bolt of pain through my left arm.

"Take that back," she said in a cool voice.

"Relax," Mom said, starting the truck.

"Take it back," Lilith said, squeezing tighter.

"Relax, Lilith!" Mom yelled.

Lilith let go of my shoulder, sat back and closed her eyes again. "Fine."

"You're lucky I'm tired, Lilith," I said, trying to ignore the fact that my left arm was now numb, "or I'd have to give you a lesson in Charlie-jitsu. And believe me, you don't want a piece of that action."

"Anytime, Charlie," she said.

"No more fighting," Mom said, backing out of the parking spot. "Lilith, chill out. Charlie, apologize to your sister and go to sleep."

"Oh, come on. We all know that Dad had a ghostwriter for the last two books. Remember that guy — Jim or Al or something? I mean, we're not going to sit around and pretend Dad's a hero or something — not after what he did."

"That's not the point, Charlie. Apologize to your sister."

I turned around and looked at Lilith. She stared back.

"Sorry."

Lilith closed her eyes and went back to meditating.

"What do you say, Lilith?" Mom said, making her way through the parking lot.

"Life is not a joke," she said.

"You might be right," I said, lying back down.

"Lilith, that's not how you accept an apology," Mom said.

"Forget it. I'm too tired for all this mumbo jumbo," I said as sleep drifted in. "How long is the drive?"

"About seven hours," Mom said.

"Wake me for lunch," I muttered, and fell fast asleep.

Friday, ?:?? p.m.

I woke up in the dark.

Alone.

With an urgent need to pee.

I was still in the truck, which was a surprise. I had some foggy memories of stopping at a McDonald's for lunch, but other than that, the whole trip was a blank.

I sat up, wiped the drool off my chin and took a look around. It was dark, but thanks to a very bright moon, it wasn't pitch-black. To my right, at about two o'clock, was a large, inn-like building — I assumed it was the inn. It was two stories high and covered in gray paint that was cracking and peeling off in spots. A sagging porch ran along the front, with a string of thick bushes covered in pink flowers growing wild against it. There were four large windows along the ground floor and six slightly smaller windows on the upper floor. From what I could see, there weren't any lights on inside. I had absolutely no idea what time it was, but that was beside the point now; what really mattered was the fact that my bladder was about to explode.

I slipped outside and took another quick look around. The gravel driveway stretched out behind the truck for about seventy-five feet before it hit the road. The other three sides of the inn were surrounded by trees, so there were plenty of places to take a whiz, but I made a beeline for the bushes growing along the front porch. I chose one that looked slightly more parched than the others and opened the floodgates.

I wouldn't normally go into too much detail about my bodily functions, but that was one of the most joyous moments of my life. Choirs of angels sang, bells rang out, trumpets blasted. I was so overwhelmed with relief that I failed to notice an old man stepping up behind me.

"Stop urinating on my roses, punk!"

He had a full head of curly gray hair and was wearing a black jacket, black pants and black gloves, but no shoes. What really caught my attention, though, was the large shotgun he was aiming at my back.

I always thought I'd panic under those kinds of circumstances, but I managed to remain surprisingly calm.

"I told you to stop urinating on my roses, punk!"

"I'd love to, but my bladder's on autopilot right now. Maybe I could just shuffle over to another bush."

"What'd you say?" he asked, squinting at me.

"I said, I'll move to another bush!"

I took a few steps to my left, and he jabbed the gun in my back.

"Don't move a gard-darn muscle! After what happened here last night, I'm well within my rights to lay you out! You got that?"

"I don't know what happened here last night, old man, but I was a long way away. My mom will vouch for me, except I'm not sure where she is at the moment."

"What'd you say?"

"I said, I wasn't here last night!"

"What?"

"I'm going to burn down all these bushes," I mumbled.

"What are you saying? Speak up," he said, jabbing me with the gun again.

"I said! I was at school last night! Choke Academy! Last night! I wasn't! Here!"

"Choke Academy? What about it?"

"I was there! I was there!"

"At Choke? Why were you at Choke?"

"That's where I go to school!"

"At Choke?" he said, lowering the gun a little. "Who are you, kid?"

"I'm Charlie. My mom is Claire. She owns this place!"

"What's your mother's name?"

"Claire!" I yelled, finally finishing up my business with the roses. "Claire Autumn!"

"Your mother is Claire Autumn?" he said, backing up a step.

"That's right. I'm Charlie!"

"You must be Charlie," he said.

"Yes," I said, turning around. "I'm Charlie."

"Yeah, I see the family resemblance now," he said, lowering the gun. "Why the hell didn't you say that in the first place, kid? Gard-darn it, you should know better than to urinate on another man's roses."

"Who are you?" I asked.

"What?"

"Who are you!"

"I'm Hal — your uncle Hal, kid," he said, looking at me like I was the crazy one. "You have to speak up. I'm a little hard of hearing."

"You don't say."

I had vague memories of an email Mom had sent a month ago about Hal still living at the inn, but she'd failed to mention that he was completely deaf and liked to wander around at night dressed all in black, carrying a shotgun.

"It's nice to meet you," I added, holding out my hand.

He looked at it like I was trying to give him a rotten fish. "You'll have to wash that thing before I shake it," he said. "Come on, I'll take you inside."

I followed him around the side of the inn, down the gravel driveway and toward the back.

"Why are you all dressed up?" I asked. "Big party? Gun convention? Shock therapy?"

"What?" he said, as we turned the back corner.

"Nothing. Where's Mom?" I shouted.

"How the heck should I know, kid?" he said, stopping in front of the back door, leaning his gun against the wall and pulling out a ring of about thirty keys.

"She's probably inside," I said, watching him try the first key in the lock. It didn't work.

"She's probably inside," he said, trying another key.

"Good thinking. By the way, how long have you been living here, Uncle Hal?" I asked. But before he could answer, a figure burst out of the trees at the back of the yard and sprinted toward us.

"Get inside!" the figure screamed, waving hands in the air. "They're right behind me!"

Hal dropped the keys, grabbed his gun and whirled around.

"Freeze!" he yelled, aiming the gun at the stranger.

"Get inside," the stranger cried, still sprinting straight at us.

"Freeze, punk!"

Our panicky visitor came to his senses and skidded to a stop about twenty feet away. He was a little on the short and scrawny side, with chin-length black hair and black-rimmed glasses. Everything he was wearing was black: military-style boots, pants and his jacket. I started to wonder if wearing black at night was a tradition in Rolling Hills.

"Please, please, please," he pleaded breathlessly. "We've got to get inside. They're right behind me."

"Who the hell are you?" Hal asked.

"I'm Miles Van Helsing. I live down the street. Please, please, please, we've got to get inside."

"What did he say?" Hal said, glancing at me.

"Just go inside," I said. "I'll explain inside!"

Hal lowered the gun, grunted something, then turned back to the door.

Miles immediately ran over to us. "Hurry!" he said, hopping from one foot to the other.

"Who's after you?" I asked, while Hal rooted through the keys.

"Hurry, hurry," Miles said, glancing over his shoulder.

Hal tried another key, but it didn't work.

"Who's after you?" I asked again, but this time Hal found the right key and opened the door. Miles pushed past both of us and dashed inside.

We followed him in, and Hal turned on the lights. We were standing in a narrow, rectangular room, with an old brown couch pushed against the opposite wall. A coffee table cluttered with newspapers and magazines was sitting in front of it. I noticed one of the newspapers was dated August 6, 1972, and there was a faded and curled *Time* magazine from 1967 with some kind of psychedelic rock band on the cover. Across from the couch, a small, ancient television was propped up on a knee-high table, its antennae reaching up in a *V*. Miles stood beside the television, peeking out of a small window that had a view of the backyard.

"Turn the lights off!" Miles hissed, crouching down. "They'll know we're here."

"What's he talking about?" Hal asked.

"He says there's someone chasing him!" I shouted. At the other end of the room was a tall bookcase, so filled with books that the shelves were sagging. Beside it was a door that I figured led into the rest of the inn. I considered marching through it and leaving Miles and Hal behind, but I didn't want to leave them unsupervised.

"I'm out of here," Hal mumbled, and he headed for the door outside. Apparently he didn't have a problem leaving *me* behind.

"No! Don't go! You've got to stop him," Miles said, grabbing my shoulders. "Please, he's in real danger."

"Look, I don't have a sweet clue what's going on right now. If you want to stop him, be my guest, but I'm staying out of it. You realize he's got a shotgun, right?"

"It's paranormal activity!" he cried, as Hal opened the door. "Humanoid creatures, three of them — very fast and very aggressive."

Either Hal didn't hear him or didn't believe him — or he just didn't care — because he went out and slammed the door shut.

"No!" Miles croaked, rushing to the door and throwing it open. "Come back! Please! It's paranormal activity!"

Hal didn't stop; he just kept clomping across the backyard, slowly disappearing into the darkness.

"Paranormal activity?" I asked.

"He could die out there."

"Go after him if you want."

Miles looked out at Hal, who was almost at the trees now, and then shut the door. "We've got to turn the lights out," he said and flicked them off.

The room went pitch-black.

"What now?" I asked. "Do we just stand here in the dark for the rest of the night?"

He didn't get a chance to answer because the door in the far corner creaked open.

"Who's there?" Miles blurted, bumping into me, and then the lights came back on.

I don't know if it was Hal's shotgun or all that talk about paranormal activity, but I was pretty worked up by that point, so I was half expecting to see a psychopath dressed in overalls and carrying a chainsaw standing on the other side of the room. Instead of a psycho, though, it was just my mom standing in the doorway, wearing green pajamas and looking tired.

"What's going on down here?" she asked.

"Oh, just standing around in the dark," I said. "By the way, thanks for leaving me out in the truck."

She wiped her eyes and yawned. "You were dead to the world when we got here, and you're too heavy for me to carry up to bed anymore, sunshine."

"A note would've been nice. Maybe a warning about Uncle Hal being mildly deranged."

"You saw Hal?"

"He let us in," Miles said.

"Who are you?" Mom asked Miles.

"I'm Miles Van Helsing," he said, hunching his way across the room and holding out his hand. "It's nice to meet you, but we've got to turn out the lights, immediately. This is an emergency."

"Why are you here?" she asked, quickly shaking his hand.

"He was chased here by paranoid creatures?" I said.

"Humanoid creatures, and from what I've seen, they're very dangerous. We really can't attract attention to ourselves," he said and then quickly reached for the switch and turned off the lights.

Mom flicked them back on.

"What's going on, Charlie?"

"I have no idea."

"Please," Miles said, reaching for the light switch again.

She covered the switch with her hand. "Do your parents know where you are?"

"My mother is aware that I'm not at home," he said.

"Well, I think now would be an excellent time to go back."

"I can't go outside, not now," Miles said, retreating across the room.

"Why is he here, Charlie?"

"Uncle Hal let him in."

"Where is Hal?"

"He's outside, possibly hunting whoever or whatever was chasing Miles."

"Please turn out the lights," Miles said.

"I'm not turning out the lights!" Mom snapped. "I'm calling your mother. What's your phone number?"

"I won't tell," Miles said. "It's too dangerous for her to be outside."

"Fine, then I guess I'll just have to call the police. Give me your phone, Charlie."

"Uh ..." I started, "I don't seem to have it anymore."

"Seriously?"

I nodded.

"That's the fourth phone you've lost this year. I swear to you, I'm not buying another one."

"Here, use mine," Miles said, pulling a cell out of his pocket. "After all, this is a public emergency and Sheriff Dutton should be informed."

"I was bluffing," Mom said. "I didn't really want to call the police."

"Too late," he said, handing her the phone. "It's already ringing."

"This is ridiculous," Mom said, but took the phone anyway.

I guess someone must have answered, because she started explaining the situation right away. When she was done, she nodded a couple of times and handed the phone back to Miles.

"The sheriff's on his way," she said. "I guess that means I'm going to have to get changed. Charlie, come with me. I'll show you up to your room."

"What about me?" Miles asked.

"You can stay here," she said. "You can even turn out the lights if you want."

I followed Mom into a larger room that had a huge, dust-coated chandelier hanging from the ceiling. Only four of its lightbulbs were still working, flickering weakly and leaving most of the room in shadows.

"That was the kids' TV room back when Hal and I were growing up, and this will be the dining room," she said. "It still needs some work."

There was a massive table, covered in a white sheet, sitting under the chandelier. It was surrounded by twelve chairs, all covered in sheets, too, making it look like we were walking in on a dinner party for ghosts. As we made our way past the table, I noticed that the wallpaper was peeling off in spots and that the floor was covered in a fine layer of dust.

From there we walked into a slightly smaller room at the front of the inn. Moonlight spilled in through two large windows. The furniture in here was covered in sheets as well, but I could guess by their size and shape that they were a collection of chairs and sofas. There was a grandfather clock in the far corner. It had stopped at two o'clock, probably a long time ago, and I wondered if it had been two in the morning or two in the afternoon.

"This will be the sitting room," she said, and then turned to our left and exited through a tall, arching doorway. I followed her out of the sitting room and into the main foyer. The front door of the inn was to my right and a wide staircase that led to the second floor on the left. Another flickering chandelier hung from the ceiling.

"That's the drawing room," she said, pointing across the foyer and into a room too dark to see into. "The sunsets are incredible to watch from in there — the light just pours in. And that," she added, pointing down a hallway that ran along beside the staircase, "leads to the kitchen."

"Where does Hal live?" I asked.

"He's converted the old servants' quarters into an apartment. It's off the kitchen, at the back, but don't go snooping around in there," she said, heading up the stairs. "He's a little eccentric."

"I noticed," I said.

The stairs to the second floor were covered in a thick red carpet and the railing was wide and solid. I was looking forward to sliding down it sometime soon.

"Hal's been living here by himself for a long time," she said, as we arrived on the second floor. "But without his cooperation, I'd never be able to do this, so give the man his privacy."

"It's on the to-do list, Ma."

"That's the master bedroom and office," she said, nodding at the door to our left. "That's where I'll be living. Your room is just down here." She led the way down a long, dark hallway to our right.

We stopped at the second door and stepped into a sleek-looking bedroom that didn't match the run-down look of the first floor at all. The walls were a dazzling white, while the floors were a dark hardwood. To my right was a dresser, and in front of me was a desk that sat under a window covered by dark wooden blinds. A black lamp, shaped like a boomerang, sat on one side of the desk, and a black vase full of fresh white flowers stood on the other. To my left was a low-lying double bed, covered with a puffy white duvet. My duffel bag was sitting at the foot of the bed, and a large black-and-white painting of a crooked old tree hung above the headboard.

"What do you think?"

"It reminds me of something."

She smiled. "You're sharper than you look, sunshine. It's an exact replica of a hotel room we stayed in when we visited Japan. All of the rooms are based on somewhere we've stayed. You're in Tokyo, and Lilith is next door in Rome."

"I'm impressed," I said, lying down on the bed. "But you're missing one thing."

"What?"

"A television. I know because I watched a whole lot of crazy Japanese cartoons the week we stayed in Tokyo."

"No TVs," she said. "I want to create a space where people can get away from things. Plus, nobody comes to Rolling Hills to watch TV. They come here for the hiking, the fishing and the slow pace, but they don't come for TV."

"What about Wi-Fi? Tell me I can get online."

"In a week we should be hooked up. Don't give me grief about this, Charlie — and don't get too comfortable. You'll have to move when the guests arrive."

"Move where?"

"I'm going to renovate the garage out back into an apartment for you and Lilith. It won't be big, but it'll be all yours."

"An apartment? You know that we already own an apartment in New York, right? And you're aware we also have a summerhouse and a winter house. I don't think we really need more places to live, Ma."

"We're selling them, Charlie."

"All of them?"

"I need a new start. We need a new start."

"What about my stuff?"

"It's in storage. I'll have it sent here when we're ready."

"Does Dad know about this? I mean, jeesh, does our whole life have to change?"

Mom was about to say something when Lilith stepped into my room. "Nothing is permanent, Charlie."

She was wearing a white full-body unitard that covered her from head to toe except for her face.

"Lilith," I said, "either you just traveled back from the future or you're about to go bobsledding."

"These are Uber-Jams, Charlie. They allow my skin to breathe while I'm asleep, leaving me more rejuvenated in the morning."

"The sheriff's coming, Lilith," Mom said. "There's a boy downstairs who refuses to leave."

"I know," Lilith grumbled, and left.

"I need to change before he gets here," Mom said. "There's pizza in the fridge if you need a snack while we wait."

"Great," I said, following her out of my room.

"The bathroom is down the hall, third door on the left."

"Thanks, but I just went."

Friday, 11:06 p.m.

I ambled back downstairs and went into the kitchen. An ancient fridge was buzzing to my left. There was a sign taped to the smaller door at the top that read: DO NOT USE THE FREEZER! I opened the bottom door and found three pieces of vegetarian pizza crammed together on a plate. The only other thing in the fridge was a small bottle of mustard. I took out the pizza and looked around for a microwave. The kitchen was big, with an old-style gas stove, a long counter that ran along the back wall, a double sink, plenty of cupboards and a wooden table in the middle with benches on either side instead of chairs, but there was no microwave. I decided I wasn't hungry enough to eat cold vegetarian pizza, so I put it back in the fridge and headed for the front door. As I passed through the foyer, Miles burst out of the darkness of the drawing room, nearly giving me a heart attack.

"Cripes, Miles, you can't jump out of a room like that," I said, trying to collect myself.

"Are you aware that there are antique dolls in there?" he said, pointing back into the drawing room. "An entire bookcase filled with antique dolls."

"Is there a problem with antique dolls?"

"Is there a problem with antique dolls?" he said. "Are you familiar with the Holscomb Affair of 1957?"

"Surprisingly no, I'm not."

"William and Judy Holscomb moved into a house at 101 Darling Street in Ogden Springs, Virginia, on June 22, 1957, with their two daughters, Georgia, who was seven, and Sally, who was five. According to investigators, William Holscomb discovered a wooden chest in the attic that had belonged to the previous owner, a Ms. Vivian Blair. Ms. Blair had resided in that house for ninety-nine years before she fell out of a third-floor window and died. Do you know what was in that chest?"

"Humanoid creatures?"

"No," he said, frowning, "it was filled with antique dolls. Neighbors told the police that they often saw Ms. Blair sitting with those dolls in front of the TV or at dinner. They chalked it up to loneliness because Ms. Blair never remarried after her first husband died. Guess what happened to him?"

"Eaten by werewolves?"

"No," Miles snapped. "He fell off a ladder when he was painting the house about six months after he'd married Ms. Blair. She mourned the death of her husband and then lived alone with those dolls until she fell out of the window. By that time, however, her house was up for sale. According to the police report, her nephew, a Mr. Norman Blair, had convinced her to move out. He had been nagging her for years to move out of the residence so that he could move in. Some people said he used the dolls against her, as proof that she was becoming senile and needed to be placed in an old-age home with proper care. Ms. Blair eventually agreed to move out, but Mr. Norman never got the chance to take up residence at 101 Darling Street."

"Let me guess," I said. "He fell off a ladder? Off the roof? Out a window?"

"No, he died of a heart attack in a Denny's restaurant about one hundred miles away. In the end, some second cousin inherited the house and put it up for sale without even looking at the place. As a result, the Holscomb family got it for a great price. It was a killer deal," he added with a smirk.

"Then the Holscombs found the chest, the dolls leaped out and slaughtered the family, yada yada yada," I said. "I think I've seen this movie three or four times."

"No, actually —" Miles started, and then there was a knock on the front door.

I turned to answer it, but Miles grabbed my arm.

"Wait," he said. "Check who it is."

"Be my guest," I said, stepping back.

Miles approached the door cautiously. "Who's there?" he called, in a slightly trembling voice.

"It's Sheriff Dutton. Is that you, Miles?"

"If you're Sheriff Dutton, what's the number on your squad car?"

"Stop playing games with me, Miles, and open the door!"

Miles turned to me, nodded and slipped back into the sitting room.

I opened the door.

Dutton was standing outside, scowling. He was a tall man with wavy brown hair and a square jaw. When he realized I wasn't Miles, he lost the scowl and smiled, flashing some seriously white teeth.

"Hello, there. I'm Sheriff Dutton," he said. "May I come in?"

"Sure," I said. "I'm Charlie."

"Nice to meet you, Charlie," he said, shaking my hand. "Where's Miles?"

"Hello, Sheriff," Miles said, stepping into the foyer.

"Time to go," Dutton said, and started toward him.

"So sorry to bother you, Sheriff Dutton," Mom said, hustling down the stairs. She'd changed into a T-shirt and jeans.

"No bother," Dutton said. "It's a pleasure to meet you in person, Mrs. Autumn."

"Ms. Autumn," she said, shaking his hand.

"I was hoping I could introduce myself under more pleasant circumstances," he said.

"That would have been nice, but this young man seems to believe that there are monsters chasing him."

Dutton shook his head. "Miles is our resident conspiracy nut. A month ago he called me about a UFO sighting out at Victor Opal's new resort."

"UFO?" I said.

"New resort?" Mom asked.

"That's right," he said. "Mr. Opal is building a five-star resort, golf course and whatnot, a few miles outside of town."

"I wasn't aware of that," Mom said, looking concerned.

"I wouldn't worry about it," Dutton reassured her, smiling. "We get our fair share of highfalutin folks in Rolling Hills, but there'll always be people coming into town who are more interested in staying at a cozy inn than some showy resort."

"I hope so," Mom said.

"I know so," Dutton said, "and if you folks are going

to get this place up and running, you'll need some sleep. Lct's hit the road, Miles."

"It's not safe out there, Sheriff. You've got to listen to me. I saw Mr. Baxter and his wife chasing —"

"Whoa, whoa," Dutton said, grabbing Miles's elbow and leading him toward the door. "These folks don't need to hear it. You can explain everything to me on the ride back home."

"But —" Miles started.

"Good evening, folks," Dutton said, putting on his hat with one hand and dragging Miles out with the other. "Sorry for the bother."

Mom and I followed him onto the porch and watched him escort Miles down the gravel walk and over to his cruiser, which was parked behind the truck.

"Lock your doors!" Miles yelled before Dutton could stuff him into the backseat.

"Ignore him!" Dutton called. "And welcome to Rolling Hills!"

"I don't see any reason to invite Miles back. Do you, Charlie?" Mom said, as Dutton backed out of the driveway.

"I don't know — he seemed to know a lot about antique dolls," I said, watching the taillights disappear.

"Excuse me?" she said, and that's when a couple of headlights appeared along the road out front, then a car peeled into the driveway, kicking up a cloud of dust.

"Expecting visitors?" I asked, as the car came to a stop behind Mom's truck.

"No," she said, sounding a little shaky. Through the

dust and the dark, I heard two car doors open and then thump shut.

"Who's that?" I asked, feeling a little shaky myself.

Two silhouettes emerged from the dust, moving toward the house.

"Um ..." Mom started, and then a familiar voice called out.

"Yo!"

"Is that ..." Mom said, squinting. "Is that Johnny?"

Johnny's my older brother. He graduated from Choke two years ago and should have gone straight to Yale. Instead, he decided to backpack around the world. At some point during his stay in Italy, he got hired as a model. While he was strutting around on catwalks, looking pretty, a TV director "discovered" him and cast him as the star of a new show called *Jaysin Night, Vampyre Hunter*. He plays an orphaned teenager, trained in kung fu by Chinese monks, who is searching for his long-lost father. The twist, of course, is that his father is a vampire, which is why he left him at the orphanage in the first place. Shockingly, it's a huge hit.

While Johnny was hugging Mom, the other person from the car walked up to me and held out her hand. She looked about my age, with red hair and green eyes. She was slim, but not slight, and was smiling at me while I stared. (I'll admit, I might have been a little smitten.)

"I'm Elizabeth," she said.

"And I'm pleased to meet you," I said.

She laughed, I laughed (I didn't know why), and we were about to shake hands when Johnny scooped me up from behind and squeezed me into a bear hug of my own.

"I'm so stoked to see you again, bro!"

"I'm tapping out, Johnny," I wheezed. "I can't breathe."

"You haven't changed a bit," he said, letting me down.

"Aren't you going to introduce me to your friend, Johnny?" Mom asked, smiling at Elizabeth.

"Oh snap. Right," he said. "Mom, this is Elizabeth. Elizabeth, this is my mom and this is my best bro, Charlie."

"You can call me Claire," Mom said, shaking Elizabeth's hand.

"You can call me Mr. Fantastic," I said. "And for the record, I'm his only brother."

"Watch out for Charlie," Johnny said, slapping me on the back. "He won't quit."

"Is Elizabeth involved with the show?" Mom asked.

"No, Ma. She picked me up."

"What?"

"He was on the side of the road," Elizabeth added.

"Excuse me?" Mom asked.

"I drove here, Ma."

"Not on your motorcycle. You know I hate that thing, Jonathan. You're going to kill yourself one of these days."

"It was smooth sailing until a couple of crazies ran onto the highway just outside of town. I managed to swerve onto the shoulder, but I blew out my back tire. Would've had to walk the rest of the way if Elizabeth hadn't stopped to give me a lift."

"Whoa, hold up a minute," I said, turning to Elizabeth. "You picked him up on the side of the road? In the dark?"

"Sure, bro," Johnny said. "It happens."

"Not in real life it doesn't," I said. "Maybe on *Jaysin Night, Vampyre Hunter*, but in real life girls driving alone, at night, don't stop and pick up strangers along the highway."

"You're Jaysin Night?" Elizabeth said, staring up at Johnny. "I can't believe I didn't recognize you."

"Well, he looks a lot smaller on TV," I said.

"What happened to your motorcycle?" Mom asked.

"Relax, everything is copacetic, Ma. Elizabeth's dad is going to take care of things."

"My dad owns the garage in town. He's going to have someone pick it up and fix the tire. Johnny can get it tomorrow afternoon — but only if I get an autograph," she added.

"You bet," Johnny said, flashing his Hollywood smile.

"What's your father's name?" Mom asked.

"Victor Opal."

"I hear he's building a new resort."

"Rolling Hills is getting popular again," Elizabeth said.

"I hope so," Mom said, glancing back at the inn. "I'd love to invite you in, but we're just finishing up the renovations, and I'm afraid the cupboards are bare at the moment."

"That's not true," I said. "We have a bottle of mustard we could share and a few slices of cold vegetarian pizza."

"Actually, it's vegan pizza," Mom said. "Lilith's gone vegan."

"She's gone a lot of other things, too," I added.

"That's all right," Elizabeth said. "It's late, and I really need to get going. It was nice meeting you."

"Give me a call when you get tired of listening to Johnny's stories about being awesome."

"Sure, Charlie," she said, and turned to leave.

Johnny followed her back to her car, which I could now see was a Porsche, although I couldn't quite make out the color in the dark. They said a few things, and then he came back carrying a backpack and his motorcycle helmet.

"I didn't think you were coming until next week," Mom said.

"Shooting wrapped up early," he said, "and I wanted to surprise you."

"That's sweet, and I'd love to hear more about your near-death experience, but I'm exhausted, and we've got a full day of work ahead of us tomorrow. We'll catch up in the morning," Mom said, heading inside.

"You bet, Ma," Johnny said. "I could use a little shut-eye."

"Yeah, I'm feeling a little tired, too," I said, stretching.

"That's impossible, Charlie," Mom said. "You spent the entire day asleep in the truck."

"It's been a hard week."

"How'd this year's Olympiad go?" Johnny asked.

"It ended abruptly."

"Show Johnny where the pizza is, and then show him up to his room," Mom said. "It's right across the hall from yours. I'm going back to bed. I'm dead on my feet."

"Sure thing, Mom. I might even dip into that bottle of mustard while I wait."

"You kill me, bro," Johnny said, as we headed for the kitchen. "You kill me."

Saturday, 8:05 a.m.

I woke up to the sound of birds squawking. I figured there must have been about a hundred of them sitting outside my window. I rolled over in bed and tried to go back to sleep, but they wouldn't let up. It was like having an alarm clock with no snooze button. After a few minutes, I got up, grumbled my way over to the window and pulled up the wooden blinds. Instead of a flock of birds, there were only three little gray feather-balls outside, standing on the edge of the roof that was overhanging the porch below. I pounded on the window, and they turned and looked up at me with their black eyes. I pounded on the glass again. They stood their ground and stared.

"I'm trying to get some sleep in here!" I shouted.

They chirped at each other a couple of times, just to irritate me, and then flew away. I watched them flap across the front yard and land in one of the huge trees growing on the other side of the lawn. Then they went back to their squawking.

I closed the blinds and was making my way back to bed when Johnny burst in.

"Rise and shine, bro!" he cried, stomping across the room and throwing open the blinds again. "Let's get some grub!"

"It's summer vacation," I said, flopping into my bed. "Why are we waking up with the freaking birds?"

"Up with the birds? You kill me, Chuck. The birds have been awake for, like, four hours. It's eight in the a.m."

"Get me some takeout and leave it outside my door.

I don't do breakfast in the summertime. I do brunch, like any civilized human being."

"Get up, Charlie, we've got work to do," Mom said, rushing in. "This is the start of our new life."

"I liked our old life," I said, putting the pillow over my head. "We stayed at resorts with room service, we slept in and we didn't renovate broken-down inns."

"Get dressed," she said, pulling the pillow away from me, "or we're going to carry you down to the truck in your underwear."

"Come on," Johnny said. "I haven't seen you since Christmas, bro. We have some serious catching up to do. Plus, I don't want to see you in your underwear. Lilith's pajamas were weird enough."

"We can do it after 10:00 a.m.," I said. "Now, make like a tree and scram!"

"It's make like a tree and *leave*, bro."

"It's too early to argue about insults. Just go!"

"Can you give us a minute alone, Johnny?" Mom asked.

"You bet, Ma," he said and left.

Mom closed the door behind him.

"Why can't we just check into a hotel?" I groaned. "At least until the renovations are done. I mean, you're not serious about *us* fixing up this place, right? I can barely tie my own shoes."

"We can't afford it, Charlie," Mom said, sitting down on the end of the bed.

"Huh?"

"There's no more money. It's all gone."

"What? That's impossible," I said, sitting up. "Dad's a

bestselling author. He's famous. I mean, he spends all his time giving those self-help, feel-good conferences to rich schmucks. He's on a round-the-world honeymoon with Mindy, for goodness' sake. The money can't just disappear overnight — we have maids and cooks to pay. They have to make a living, you know."

"First of all, we didn't lose it overnight. Your dad made a lot of bad investments, he wasn't paying his taxes and there were a whole bunch of shady deals that I'm not even going to get into. Trust me, it's all gone. And, for the record, he's not on his honeymoon. Mindy left him when she found out about the money problems. Now he's kind of on the run, I guess. It's bound to come out in the news any day."

"But you must have money from the divorce?"

"Not as much as you'd think," she said. "And I sunk most of it into this place. So it's kind of important for you to get up and help out. This inn is all we have left."

"What about your family's money?"

"My dad was a softy and not very savvy when it came to business. The money he inherited from my grandfather kind of slipped through his fingers. If you want a new phone, then you're going to earn it."

"That's harsh, Ma."

"That's reality, Charlie."

"Do Johnny and Lilith know?"

"I'll tell Johnny today," she said, "but I don't want you to tell Lilith yet. She idolizes your father, and I don't know how she's going to take this."

"Not well," I said, sitting up. "Does this mean I won't be going back to Choke?"

"I'm afraid so."

"Can I burn my uniforms?"

"I wouldn't. You'll need something to wear until your clothes arrive."

Saturday, 8:22 a.m.

I threw on a wrinkled white shirt, wrinkly khakis, a pair of slightly stinky brown socks and my student handbook-approved dress shoes, then grabbed my toothbrush and headed for the bathroom at the end of the hall.

The bathroom renovations were only half done. Most of the yellow-white tiles on the floor were cracked, and the old-fashioned tub, which had paws on the ends of its stubby legs, looked grimy, but the sink and toilet were shiny and new. I brushed my teeth, did my business and headed downstairs.

Lilith's door was closed as I strolled back down the hallway, but I could imagine her room being so neat and tidy it would be impossible to tell a human being had ever been inside. Johnny's door was wide open, on the other hand, and it was so messy it looked like he'd been attacked by something during the night. His bag was lying in the middle of the floor, clothes spilling out of it, the sheets and blankets from the bed were crumpled in balls on the floor, and two pillows were propped at the bottom of the door, apparently to keep it open. It was so cluttered, I couldn't even guess what hotel room Mom was trying to copy.

At the top of the stairs, I considered sliding down the banister. It felt solid enough, but I didn't want to risk it collapsing, so I went down the old-fashioned way. I was going to go straight outside but stopped and glanced into the drawing room instead. There were two large windows along the front, with a variety of sofas and chairs lining the walls, and in the far corner was a baby grand piano. The wall to my immediate left was covered by a floor-to-ceiling bookshelf, only the shelves didn't contain books — there were antique dolls on them, all sitting in rows, staring into the room with their shiny, empty eyes. Most of them were wearing frilly dresses and had tiny, puckered smiles and abnormally long eyelashes. Some of them had fancy hats, with bows and ribbons hanging off the brims, propped on their heads. How long had they all been sitting there, staring? Twenty years? Fifty? I was just adding *get rid of dolls* to the top of my mental to-do list when my stomach grumbled.

It was hot when I stepped outside, and a million crickets were chirruping in the long grass, almost drowning out the squawking of the birds that were back outside my bedroom window.

"Hurry up, bro!" Johnny yelled from the truck. "I'm starving."

Johnny was in the front, and Lilith shuffled over as I squeezed into the back.

"There must be a million crickets in the grass. That sound could drive a man batty," I said, sliding in.

"They're cicadas, not crickets," Lilith said.

"Whatever. They're bugs and they're loud," I said, as Mom backed out of the driveway. "By the way, that's some collection of dolls in the drawing room."

"They belonged to my great-grandmother. They're extremely valuable."

"They're extremely creepy," Johnny said.

"They're antiques."

"They're still creepy, Ma," Johnny added, and we started down the street.

Elm Street is one of those old country roads that looks like it's just about to be overrun by the trees on either side and is covered in long cracks that run through it like veins.

"In episode seven of *Vampyre Hunter*," Johnny said as we drove along, "I had to deal with a horde of possessed dolls. By the time we wrapped up shooting, I was totally freaked out."

"I'd be careful, Johnny," I said. "According to Miles Van Helsing, those things are vicious."

"Miles Van who?" Johnny asked.

"Forget it," Mom said. "Great-grandma Autumn's dolls aren't possessed."

"They've been sitting there, alone, for a long time," I said. "Maybe they've, you know, awoken. No wonder Hal walks around with a shotgun."

"You might be right, bro," Johnny said. "The research dude on our show says there's a lot of weird stuff that goes on in the world that can never be explained, like frogs raining down or people randomly bursting into flames."

"Are you still wearing your uniform?" Lilith asked, cutting into our conversation. For the record, Lilith was decked out in skin-tight black running pants, a high-tech black running shirt and black and yellow sneakers with individual toes.

"Lilith, unlike you, I don't strut around in thermodynamic pajamas or a running outfit that looks like it was built for Catwoman. Plus, Sterling forces me to wear a uniform when I arrive at Choke, I'm forced to wear it every stinking day that I'm there, and he makes sure I'm wearing one when I leave, so I don't see the point in packing civilian clothes."

"You pack them because, eventually, you'll go on summer vacation," she said. "Like Dad said in his book *The Way of the Wise*, the prudent warrior always plans ahead."

"Sometimes the prudent warrior doesn't have a strong grasp of reality," I mumbled.

"You're the one talking about dolls coming to life, Charlie. I'd say you're the one losing your grasp of reality."

"Reality can be surprising," I said, "and sometimes people aren't what you think they are, Lilith."

"Charlie," Mom snapped, "that's enough."

"Right ... fine," I said, biting my lip, "I guess I wasn't expecting to be exiled to the edge of the world for the summer without access to my clothes." A big part of me wanted to tell Lilith that Dad wasn't the glowing superhero she thought he was, but I'd promised Mom that I'd keep it under wraps, so I kept my mouth shut and looked out the window.

"You look ridiculous," Lilith mumbled.

"Guilty as charged," I said. "But at least my teeth are clean."

"Did you use the sink in the upstairs bathroom? You know there's something wrong with the plumbing, right?

Mom thinks the water might be contaminated," Lilith said.

"Contaminated?" I asked, running my tongue along my teeth. "Mom, you didn't tell me that."

"It's not contaminated," Mom said, coming to a stop sign at the end of Elm Street. "There was something wonky with the water pressure, so I called the plumber, and he's coming this afternoon. The pipes are pretty old, and until he figures it out, we'll have to avoid having showers. We probably shouldn't drink or brush our teeth with it either. I'll buy some bottled water today."

"I already brushed my teeth," I said, and tried to roll down the window in the back, but it wouldn't open.

"Mom, undo the child-lock. I need to spit."

"Relax," Mom said, taking a right off Elm Street and starting down Oak Avenue. "It's nothing to worry about. Plus, we'll be there in a minute."

"Contaminated is a worry, Mom. Let me roll down the window. I need to spit."

"I'm not driving into town with you spitting out the window, Charlie."

By now, houses were appearing on our left and right. They were big old country houses with front porches, huge lawns and white picket fences.

"Please, I think I'm dying back here."

"Didn't you say there was toilet water mixed up with the sink water, Mom?" Lilith asked.

"Do you want me to throw up?" I said, turning to Lilith. "Because I'll throw up all over you if that's what you want."

"That's not true, Charlie," Mom said.

"In episode nine of *Vampyre Hunter*, I ended up in a

town where all the residents had been changed into zombies because of contaminated drinking water," Johnny chimed in. "I got to use a crossbow in that episode. It was totally rad."

"Open the window!" I cried.

"We're almost there," Mom snapped, as we reached a three-way intersection at the bottom of Oak Avenue. Across the street, directly in front of us, was a garage.

"There she is," Johnny said, pointing at a black and red motorcycle that looked like it could probably go about a thousand miles an hour. "I guess they haven't had a chance to fix it," he mumbled.

"I really need to spit," I said, as we made a right onto Church Street, which was obviously the main drag in Rolling Hills, judging by the number of people who were already milling around. "I need to purge!"

"We're almost there," Mom said.

"Where is there?" I asked.

"Here," she said, and pulled up to the curb next to a restaurant called Romero's.

I threw open the door, jumped out and started spitting like crazy all over the sidewalk.

Saturday, 8:32 a.m.

Romero's was housed in the same type of brick-front, two-story building that lined both sides of Church Street. Sure, there were little differences: the awning at Romero's had white and green stripes and the one next door had yellow and red stripes, and some of the places didn't have awnings at all, but by and large, Church Street consisted of the same neat and tidy building repeated again and again.

"It hasn't changed a bit since I was a kid," Mom said, getting out of the truck.

Church Street was about five blocks long, and at the end was a red brick church, with a tall white steeple jutting, like a giant needle, straight into the sky. Black iron lampposts arced over the street, and the occasional maple tree stood here and there. The sidewalks looked clean enough to eat off of. Well, they were clean enough to eat off of until I spat all over them.

Mom stopped admiring the view and turned to me. "Charlie, this isn't the kind of town where you just spit all over the sidewalk."

"I'll make sure to do it in the road the next time I brush my teeth with toilet water."

"Let's just get something to eat," Johnny said, and we all filed into Romero's.

The place was filled with old-timers eating big platefuls of bacon and eggs and sipping from steaming mugs of coffee. Mom insisted we sit at the front counter, just like she and Hal used to do when they were kids. The locals stared at us as we made our way to the stools and took a seat.

A few seconds after we sat down, our waitress — a husky woman with gray hair and a name tag that read *Mabel* pinned to her white shirt — bustled over. She handed out the menus and filled our cups with coffee without asking if we wanted any.

"Back in a sec," she said and left.

"Try the blueberry pancakes," Mom said. "They're delicious."

"I don't know," I said, looking around. "I think we might get run out of town if we don't order the bacon and eggs."

"I'll get both," Johnny said, putting his menu down.

"Don't you have to watch your figure for your fans?" I asked.

"The producers want me to beef up a bit for next season, so I've got to increase my calorie intake."

"They want you to beef up, Johnny, not pork up."

"Don't worry about me, bro," he said. "I've got some killer workouts that'll keep me a lean, mean, vampire-fighting machine. You should join me, Chuck, you're looking a little soft in the middle."

"The Ping-Pong coach at Choke likes me to carry around a little extra weight, you know, for reserve energy, in case I get caught in an extra-long match."

"We didn't have a Ping-Pong team at Choke, did we?" Johnny asked, but before I could explain, Sheriff Dutton walked in and strolled over.

"Morning," he said, nodding at us.

"Good morning, Sheriff," Mom said, swiveling around on her stool.

"Please, call me Rick."

"As long as you call me Claire. Catch any monsters last night?" she said, grinning.

"Can't say that I did, but I had my hands full. There were plenty of calls. Some of the local kids were out celebrating the end of the school year."

"Speaking of trouble, I'm not sure my brother, Hal, came back home last night. Do you think he's okay?"

"Well, you know Hal, he's a ... little eccentric, if you don't mind my saying so."

"It's just the truth," Mom said.

"But he knows the woods around these parts better than most folks," he added, and took a business card and pen out of his pocket. He scribbled a number on the back and handed it to Mom. "If he's not back by dinner tonight, give me a call and I'll see what I can do."

"Thanks," Mom said.

"What can I get you, Sheriff?" Mabel asked, wandering back with her pot of coffee.

"I'll have a big cup of joe and some blueberry flapjacks," Dutton said. "You all have a good day," he added and then took a seat at a booth in the back.

"He's a handsome devil, isn't he?" Mabel said, winking at Mom. "And he's single, too, if you can believe it."

"Do you have any vegan options?" Lilith blurted.

"Eggs?" Mabel said, shrugging.

Lilith frowned. "I'll have a bowl of oatmeal, please — no milk."

"I'd like the bacon and eggs — and could you put some extra bacon on the side?" I said, looking pointedly at Lilith.

"I'll see what I can do," Mabel said, while Lilith glared at me. "It'll be a bit of a wait — we're a little backed up today. One of our waitresses called in sick. I think she came down with a bad case of celebrating the end of school."

Mabel wasn't joking. It was almost an hour before we got our food. While we waited, Mom went over some of the renovation plans and assigned a few jobs. She'd hired some locals to handle most of the work, but we'd be helping out with a bit of the painting, the mowing and the general tidying up of the place. She said it was the perfect opportunity for some family bonding.

Spending my days doing manual labor with my family sounded like about as much fun as hanging out with Stanley Peck back at Choke for the entire summer, so when everyone piled into the truck after breakfast to go pick out paint, I convinced Mom I needed to peruse the shops on Church Street for some new clothes.

There weren't any of the usual clothing stores or fast-food joints along Church Street. They were all local operations with names like Frog Brothers Café, Rosemary's Roses or Eats Like a Bird Sandwich Shoppe. In fact, the only clothing store I saw was called Chaney's Fine Garments, and it looked like it sold clothes that were made sometime in the mid-1940s. I needed new clothes, but not that badly, so I decided to wait for my stuff to arrive.

The only place on the street that really stood out was a restaurant called The Opal. The front was all sleek steel and glass instead of brick, and it was twice as wide as the stores around it. More importantly, one of the cars parked out front was a shiny red Porsche. I decided to saunter over and casually press my face against the restaurant's front window to see if Elizabeth was inside, but before I had a chance to make myself look like a crazy stalker, she strolled out the front door with a tall man dressed in a gray suit and wearing a fedora.

"Hi, Charlie," she said, smiling. She had her hair tied

back in a ponytail and was wearing cut-off shorts and a white tank top.

"Wow, what a surprise," I said. "I didn't expect to see you here."

"This is my dad," she said, gesturing toward the older man. He was probably a few inches over six feet and had the kind of tanned, chiseled face that you only expect to see on mountain climbers or people who have sailed around the world a couple of times. I could see that his hair under the fedora was black with streaks of gray.

"Dad, this is Charlie Harker. He's Johnny's brother."

"Mr. Opal," I said, shaking his hand, which was massive and looked like it could crush mine if he sneezed the wrong way. His grip was surprisingly limp, though, and his skin felt clammy.

"Charlie," he said, staring down at me from behind a pair of aviator sunglasses.

"Dad's not feeling well. I'm sending him home."

"It's nothing," Opal said in a flat voice.

"Sounds like something's going around," I said. "I just spent an hour at Romero's waiting for my breakfast because one of the waitresses called in sick."

"Our maître d' is sick, too," she said, looking a little concerned.

"It's just a head cold. It's nothing," Opal said, still staring at me. I saw myself reflected in the silver sheen of his glasses and thought I looked like a person who'd been living on the streets for a few weeks.

"It's probably a migraine," Elizabeth said, as Opal headed for a black Mercedes. "He could barely walk when he woke up this morning, but he seems to be getting better. At least he *says* he's feeling better."

"I am feeling better," Opal added drily, getting into his car.

"I'm going to follow him home," she said, as he started up the car and pulled away, "just to make sure he makes it okay." She was about to get into her Porsche but stopped and added, "Say hi to Johnny for me, okay?"

"Sure. Will do," I said, smiling like an idiot and giving her a thumbs-up. This was the story of my life. In any town we'd ever visited, some girl (or girls) would fall for Johnny, and I'd end up relaying their messages to him. I'm not going to deny it was slightly annoying to be consistently overlooked for my golden-boy older brother, but what really cooked my craw was when they started cutting into my nap time, or my floating-in-the-pool time, or my lying-in-the-hammock-doing-nothing time to pick my brain about what Johnny was "really like" or ask if he'd been talking about them around the dinner table. I was hoping it didn't come to that with Elizabeth Opal.

She drove away, and I continued my walk along Church Street. I wandered past a few more stores and then spotted a knee-high chalkboard, propped up against a wall at the mouth of a narrow alley that ran between Brooks Books and R. Sterling's Fine Jewelry. Scrawled across the board in yellow letters were the words *Voodoo Juice Bar*. Under them, a yellow arrow pointed into the alley. I figured an establishment that was located in an alley was the perfect place for a fine young man like myself to escape family bonding time, so I headed down to check it out.

There were a few other arrows, drawn on the walls and along the ground, that pointed the way past the back of Brooks Books, around a corner and into another alley. That's where I found a green wooden door held open with a brick. There was no sign above the door, but there was an arrow on the ground, pointing inside. So, I followed it in.

The walls in the Voodoo Juice Bar were deep purple, and the only light in the place was coming from a bare lightbulb hanging from the middle of the ceiling. There were three tables, surrounded by folding lawn chairs, and a ragged-looking couch pushed into the back corner. The bar was on the other side of the room, and there were shelves stacked behind it, packed with jars, boxes, shakers, vials and beakers. One of the larger jars had five or six tarantulas inside, floating around in a clear, thick-looking liquid. Above the shelves was a blackboard with about fifty different drinks scrawled across it in yellow chalk. The drinks had names like Pinpricks, Zombaid, Undead-Colada, The Vortex and my personal favorite, The Re-Animator. I was still scanning the list when a man's head poked through a set of red beads hanging from the doorframe of a back room. He had white hair that puffed off his head like a fluffy cloud and was wearing black-tinted goggles over his eyes.

"What are you here for?" he blurted.

"Uh ... a drink, I think?"

"What? Why are you here? What's your name?"

"His name is Charlie," a voice said from behind me.

I turned and saw Miles Van Helsing standing in the

doorway. He looked like he was wearing the same black clothes as the night before, only now he had on a black baseball cap.

"He's okay, Dr. Vortex," Miles added, coming toward me.

"I'm not sure you're qualified to make that kind of judgment call, Miles," I said.

"Trust me, Doctor," Miles said, pulling a twenty out of his pocket and laying it down on the bar, "he's clean."

"What'll you have?" Vortex asked, stepping out from behind the red beads. He was lean and tall, and wore a pair of big black rubber gloves and a white lab coat.

"We'll take two Re-Animators," Miles answered.

"That doesn't have any spiders in it, does it?" I asked.

"Just the fangs," Vortex said, staring at me from behind those black goggles.

My eyebrows shot up.

"He's joking, Charlie," Miles said, slapping me on the back. "Let's have a seat."

"Good, because spider venom this early in the morning gives me a headache."

Vortex pulled the goggles down and smiled. His eyes were a brilliant blue. "Me, too," he said and started grabbing jars off the shelf behind him.

"Dr. Vortex is a genius," Miles said, leading me to one of the tables in the back. I sat down in a lawn chair across from him. "He's a scientist, a brilliant inventor, and he makes the best drinks in town. On top of that, he could help us out of this mess."

"What mess?"

"Were you not listening to me last night?"

"The sheriff said it was just some local kids blowing off steam."

"He's wrong," Miles said, as Vortex started a blender behind the bar.

"Is this just some prank you play on all the new kids in town?"

"This situation is as far from a prank as you can possibly get."

The blender stopped, and Vortex brought over two large jars filled with a greenish-brown mixture. He put them down and left, disappearing behind the beads and into the back room.

I sniffed my drink. It smelled like dirt.

"It tastes better than it smells," Miles said.

"Better than dirt? I find that hard to believe."

He grabbed his, gulped back half the glass and slammed it back onto the table. "You'll just have to trust me."

I nodded and took a sip. He was right; it tasted a whole lot better than it smelled.

"I'm not crazy," he said.

"No, you're right. It kind of tastes like a Creamsicle mixed with —"

"I'm not talking about the drink, Charlie. I'm talking about last night. I'm not crazy — there's something highly irregular going on with our mutual neighbor, Mr. Ted Baxter."

"I don't suppose he's connected with the antique dolls you told me about?"

"The antique dolls?"

"That stuff about the Holscombs. I didn't hear how it all turned out."

"Oh, right. Well, they hadn't been seen for a few days, so the cops took a look inside. All the clothes were folded and put away, the fridge was full of food, the TV was on, et cetera, et cetera, but there was no sign of the Holscombs. They found the dolls tucked under the covers of Mr. and Mrs. Holscomb's bed ... But forget about that. The Baxters are the immediate problem here."

"So, you actually think the dolls murdered the entire Holscomb family? And then what did they do? Bury them in the backyard?"

"Forget about the Holscombs, would you!" Miles said. "We can go into the long and sordid history of antique doll murders some other time. Right now, I need you to focus on the Baxters."

"Okay, fine," I said, taking a bigger sip. "I'll stay clear of Mr. Baxter. Consider me warned."

"No, no, no," he said, "I'm not talking about staying away from the man. I'm talking about *doing* something about this situation. Do you understand me?"

"Not exactly," I said and took another sip. I was starting to think that Dr. Vortex's Re-Animator might be the most delicious thing I'd ever tasted.

"Last night," he said, leaning in, "at 8:58 p.m., I was finishing up my nightly ten-mile run —"

"You should be talking to my sister," I said.

"I think it's important to stay fit for emergency situations."

"So does she."

"Just listen."

"My apologies," I said and nearly finished off the Re-Animator in one big gulp.

"I was finishing up my run when I noticed a man, dressed in a navy blue suit, sprinting through Mr. Baxter's backyard," he said, and looked at me like this should mean something.

"Uh-huh."

"Don't you see? Adults in suits don't sprint through other people's backyards unless they are highly motivated."

"Highly motivated?"

"Exactly," he said.

"Highly motivated by what?"

"Now you're asking the right questions," he said, smiling. "I didn't have to wait long to find out because about three seconds after the man in the suit ran by, Mr. Baxter and his wife emerged from the corner of the house, chasing after him toward the rear of their property. And do you know what they were wearing?"

I shook my head and considered getting another Re-Animator.

"Their pajamas," he said triumphantly.

"Their pajamas?"

"Don't you see? Pajama-wearing adults do not chase suit-wearing adults through their backyards — it just doesn't happen. Mr. Baxter wasn't even wearing a shirt, just some blue pajama pants. And Mrs. Baxter was wearing a pink housecoat and pink fuzzy slippers. And, even if pajama-wearing people did start chasing suit-wearing people off their properties every night of the week, it wasn't just what they were wearing that was significant, it was how they were moving that really stood out."

"How were they moving?"

"They were moving at an incredible velocity," he said, his eyes getting wide. "If I didn't know better, I would've guessed they were Olympic sprinters on some powerful, performance-enhancing drug. But they didn't have the smooth movements of trained athletes — they were kind of jerking, like they were being pulled along by invisible strings."

"And they were chasing the man in the suit?"

"That's the kicker," he said. "This man was extremely large. I would estimate he was at least six and a half feet tall and muscular. He was bigger than Mr. and Mrs. Baxter put together, but he was scared of them, really scared. I saw his face before he ran into the woods behind the property, and he looked terrified."

"Well, that's a scary story, Miles," I said, getting up. "Good luck with everything. If I see Mr. and Mrs. Baxter running around in their underwear, I'll be sure to get out of the way."

"Their pajamas," he said, standing up, too. "Look, I'm telling you this because we need to do something. We need to warn people!"

"I'll put it at the top of my to-do list," I said.

"You don't get it," he said, shaking his head in frustration. "Look, later that night I went back to investigate the situation. I hid in one of the trees at the rear of the Baxter property and observed the house. At precisely 10:48, Baxter came out of his house and walked to the small barn at the back of his property. When he came out, Mrs. Baxter and the man in the suit were following him. They were walking in single file."

"Wow, single file — that's pretty weird, Miles."

"That's what I thought," he said, "but it gets worse. They heard me, I don't know how, I was thirty yards away, staying perfectly still, but they heard me. About halfway to the house, they all stopped walking at exactly the same time and turned around. I don't have any definitive proof, but I'd say they're sharing what is commonly referred to as a hive mind. They stopped, turned and then, without saying a word, they started marching toward me. That's when I took some serious evasive action, my friend, and a few minutes later I was trying to explain what happened to you and your uncle."

"I'll make sure I stay on my toes, Miles," I said, heading for the door. "Thanks for the drink."

"Did your uncle come home?" he asked, just as I was walking out.

"I don't think so," I said.

"I think he knows something is wrong, Charlie. That's why he left. He knows."

"Sure," I said, and left Miles standing in the middle of the Voodoo, looking worried.

I headed back to Church Street, which was still busy. It wasn't New York City–busy, not by a long shot, but it had a certain bustle about it. It was a relief to see there were a few people around under the age of fifty. There were even a few under the age of eighteen, but I didn't feel much like making friends, not in my slightly ripe Choke clothes. So I headed back to the inn.

About two minutes into the hike up Oak Avenue, I realized they should have called this town Tall and Steep

Hills instead of Rolling Hills. It hadn't seemed like Oak was straight up and down when we were driving in the truck, but it was a different kettle of fish when you were on foot. The fact that the day had quickly gone from mildly hot to scorching wasn't helping matters — and as delicious as the Re-Animator had tasted, it wasn't doing much in the way of Re-Animating me. I would have curled up and turned into a puddle of goo on one of the big front yards, but I thought it would reflect badly on Mom, so I kept trudging onward and upward, withering away a little with every step.

Saturday, 10:35 a.m.

By the time I staggered back into the driveway, I was soaked in sweat. I kind of noticed the beat-up red pickup truck parked beside the inn, and some part of me realized there were four men sitting on the steps of the front porch, but I was too exhausted to really care.

"Kind of hot," one of the men said, standing up as I wobbled toward him. He was tall, dressed in jeans and a T-shirt, but that was pretty much all I registered.

"I've seen hotter," I said and wiped the sweat off my face with my shirt.

"I'm Jake," he said, holding out his hand. "Jake Steel. We're helping out with the renovations."

"Charlie," I said, pushing past him, stepping around the other three and lying down in the shade of the front porch.

"Is your mom around?"

"Paint ..." I mumbled.

"What?" he asked, but luckily that's when Mom pulled into the driveway. I was too tired to answer any more questions.

"It was nice to meet you, kid," he said, and walked away.

I heard Mom introducing Lilith and Johnny to Jake, and then they headed back my way.

"This is my other son, Charlie," she said.

I opened my eyes a crack. Jake, his three helpers and Mom were standing over me.

"We've met," Jake said, smiling.

"Charlie, get up," Mom barked. "I need you to help Johnny and Lilith put the paint cans in the cellar."

"Just give me two more minutes," I said.

"Up!"

Using every ounce of my will, I sat up and wiped the sweat out of my eyes. Jake and his crew, who were all men who looked like they'd enjoy shoveling rocks just for kicks and giggles, shuffled by in dusty work boots. That's when I noticed a fifth man who was with them. He was leaning against the wall by the front door, deep in the shade. He was wearing the same kind of dusty boots as the others but was wrapped up in a black jacket with the hood up. I started to sweat more just looking at him. Under the hood, he was wearing a Boston Red Sox ball cap, the brim pulled low, and under the hat he had on a pair of black wraparound sunglasses. He stared at me for a few seconds and then went inside after the others.

"Get up, Charlie," Lilith said, walking by with two cans of paint in each hand and going inside, too.

"Bro," Johnny called from the back of the truck, "get over here and grab some cans!"

"Easy does it, Johnny," I said, getting up and dragging myself over to the back of the pickup. "Not all of us ate a five-thousand-calorie breakfast."

"You could use the exercise, Chuck."

"There's got to be thirty cans of paint back here," I said, looking into the back of the truck.

"Thirty-five," Johnny said.

He handed me a can, and I started back toward the front door.

"Seriously, you can handle more than one, right?"

"I need a bit of a warm-up," I said. "I don't want to pull any muscles."

Johnny passed me on the way to the porch. He was carrying three cans of paint in each hand, but the front door was closed, so he had to stop and wait.

"You see," I said, opening the door, "it's a good thing I kept one hand free. Otherwise you'd be stuck out here for who knows how long."

"You're a genius, bro," he said, marching inside and down the hallway to the kitchen.

"Sarcasm isn't your thing, John-John," I said, following behind him. "Leave that to me and Lilith."

"What?" Lilith grumbled. She was standing in the far corner of the kitchen, in front of a door that was only about four feet high. The paint cans she'd been carrying were at her feet, and she was holding a flashlight.

"Did those cans get too heavy for you, Lilith?" I asked.

"I've finished four triathlons this year, Charlie. I think I can handle it."

"Did you carry any paint cans during your precious triathlons?"

She frowned and handed me the flashlight. "Here — you have an extra hand."

"And a good thing, too," I said. "Otherwise, who would be here to carry flashlights and open doors?"

Lilith growled a little, opened the door and then picked up her paint cans. "After you," she said, nodding into the darkness.

I turned the flashlight on and aimed it inside. About twelve wooden planks, masquerading as stairs, led down to a dirt floor. The ceiling over the stairs was only slightly higher than the door, maybe five feet high, and the walls were so close together that Johnny and Lilith would have to walk sideways in order to get the cans down the stairs. It looked more like a narrow chute than a stairway.

"Move it, bro," Johnny said, nudging me forward.

"How long since anyone's been down there?" I asked.

"Go!" Lilith barked, and pushed forward until I was forced to step through the door and onto the first stair. It creaked and bent a little under my foot, but it didn't break.

"I don't think we should —" I started, but they were pressing in from behind, so I had to keep going.

I moved quickly, the stairs groaning under me, and was surprised when I reached the bottom without a broken ankle. It smelled like dirt down there, but it was damp and cool, which was a nice break from the heat.

"Well," I said, "I guess we can leave the cans here."

"Not here," Lilith said. "We keep going until we get to a door."

"Yeah, Mom gave me the key," Johnny added.

"And you're going to follow orders like a good little Johnny, aren't you?"

"Keep moving!" Lilith barked.

I shuffled down the passage for about twenty feet before I had to take a left. The stone walls seemed like they were closing in on us ever so slightly with each step. By the time we finally arrived at an ancient-looking wooden door, I was feeling a little cramped and a whole lot claustrophobic.

"Do you have the key?" I asked.

There was no way for Johnny to squeeze by me, so he handed it over. The key was long, made out of iron or steel and felt cool and significant in my hand. I'd just slipped it into the keyhole, when a small herd of mice darted across my foot and went squealing down the passage behind us.

"I think we're going to need to buy a cat or three before the guests arrive," I said.

"Just open the door," Lilith snapped.

I opened it, and we shuffled into a room that felt big. I couldn't really tell how big because it was pitch-black inside, except for a thin slash of light that seemed to be floating in the far right corner. Below it, the dirt floor was cut by a similar slash of light.

"That's got to be the door to the backyard," Lilith said, putting her cans down and snatching the flashlight out of my hand.

"Why didn't we just come in there?" I asked.

"Because it's bolted from the inside," Johnny said, dropping his cans and following Lilith.

"Of course it is," I said, putting down my can of paint and starting after them.

Unfortunately, Johnny and Lilith had hustled across the room so quickly I was left mostly in the dark and ended up running into a wooden box, cracking my shin. I limped to the side, tripped over another box and fell. I landed sideways on something metal and rolled onto the dirt floor, gasping for air.

"You okay, bro?" Johnny called.

"No," I wheezed.

"Hold on a sec," Johnny said, and the doors opened.

The slash of light turned into a giant square of sunshine and I saw I was surrounded by boxes, old furniture and stacks of dusty books. The metal thing I'd landed on was part of an old bed frame.

"You hurt, Charlie?" Johnny said, rushing over.

"I'm good," I said, sitting up. "I just need to take a breather for a few hours."

"Suck it up, Chuck," Lilith called, starting out of the cellar. "Those paint cans aren't going to move themselves."

"Need a hand?" Johnny asked and offered to help me up.

"Give me a second."

"Sure, bro," he said and went outside, too.

"I'm right behind you," I called.

I eased my way up, wincing a little, and was about to head outside when I noticed a wooden trapdoor in the floor a few feet to my left. The dirt around it had obviously been scuffed up recently and the iron ring that was sitting in the middle had a rope tied to it that looked brand-new. I was heading over for a closer look when Lilith arrived with four more cans of paint.

"Move it, Charles," she said, "or I'm going to make sure all your best buds back at Choke know that you make your little sister do all the heavy lifting."

"Why do you think they need a cellar under a cellar?" I asked.

"Quit stalling," she said, dropping the cans.

"I admit it, Lilith, this would normally be an excellent stalling tactic, but I'm legitimately curious," I said, but she was gone, and Johnny was on his way in with six more cans of his own.

"We could use a hand, bro."

"Sure," I said, adding *find out what's under the cellar* to my mental to-do list.

Saturday, 11:05 a.m.

After we finished with the paint cans, I went back to my room and changed into some clothes that weren't drenched in my own sweat. Unfortunately, the only things I had in the ball of dirty clothes I'd stuffed into my bag back at Choke, besides khaki pants and white shirts, were my blue gym shorts and a matching blue tank top, with *CHOKE* printed across the front in thick white letters. I must have left my sneakers back at school, and I didn't really want to traipse around in dress shoes and shorts, so I rolled back outside in a pair of worn-down flip-flops I'd stashed at the bottom of the bag.

"Looking good, bro," Johnny said when I stepped onto the front porch. "Coach is out back. He says calisthenics start in five minutes."

"Sounds good," I said. "That'll be a lot more fun than moving paint cans with you two."

"You only moved five cans," Lilith said. She was sitting cross-legged on the front lawn.

"Sure, but they were the heaviest ones," I said. "Plus, I was just getting warmed up. What's next?"

"Scraping," Mom said, coming outside. "There's a high-pressure water sprayer in the back of Jake's truck. Johnny will be in charge of that."

"Why does the TV star get the cushy job? Did he bribe you?" I asked.

"Yes, and he paid a lot more than you can afford. Where are your shoes, Charlie?"

"I've temporarily misplaced them, and I refuse to wear brown dress shoes with shorts — not until after Labor Day, anyway."

"You kill me, bro," Johnny said, laughing as he headed for Jake's truck.

"Here," Mom said, handing me and Lilith a paint scraper each. "I'll call you in for lunch."

Johnny got busy hosing the paint off using the high-pressure sprayer, while Lilith and I took off the leftovers with our scrapers. About ten minutes into the job, I was drenched again, in a combination of sweat and the blowback from Johnny's sprayer. Five minutes after that, my arms felt like wet noodles, and my shoulders were starting to cramp up. Pieces of gray-white paint were sticking to me like giant flakes of dandruff, and I was seriously considering taking a break, when Johnny turned the sprayer off, the engine rumbled to a stop and I heard a high-pitched whine coming from somewhere down the road.

"What's that sound?" Johnny asked.

"I'm not sure," I said, taking a few steps toward the road. It sounded like a lawn mower engine that was about to explode, and it was getting closer.

"Sounds like a —" Johnny started, and then Miles roared into the end of our driveway on a miniature motorcycle, about half the size of a regular motorcycle, that looked like a bunch of old pipes, pieced together. He left the asphalt, hit the gravel, skidded, straightened out and then shot into the front yard. I ran to the corner of the inn just in time to see him hit something hidden in the grass and go flying over his handlebars.

"Snap!" Johnny said, running up beside me.

"Miles?" I yelled.

Miles sat up and shook his head, like he was trying to clear some water out of his ear.

"Are you okay?" I asked, running over to him. His minicycle was lying about ten feet behind him in the grass, wedged up against a large branch that had fallen off of one of the trees.

"I need to buy a helmet," he said. He looked a little dazed, but other than that, he seemed fine.

"That was a humongous wipeout, dude," Johnny said, helping him up.

"I'm okay," he said, shaking his head.

"What are you doing here?" I asked.

"I wanted to see if your uncle came back."

"I don't think he did."

"I need to find out what happened to him last night."

I wiped a few flakes of paint off my arm and stretched out my shoulders. They felt shaky. Summer was not supposed to be about getting covered in paint chips and working until your shoulders were quivering uncontrollably. Summer was a time for sleeping and swimming and watching three really bad horror movies back to back to back. Summer was a time when you should be able to go check on your crazy uncle Hal, just to make sure he was okay.

"You know, Miles," I said, turning around, "that's an excellent idea. I'm taking a quick break, everyone."

Lilith, who had been standing a few feet behind us, stepped in front of me. "Hal didn't come back."

"Miles, this is my sister, Lilith."

"Hi," Miles said, but Lilith didn't look at him.

"He didn't come back."

"You can't know that for sure, Lilith."

"I do."

"Well, I'm going to check on him, just the same. So, if you'll kindly excuse me," I said, brushing past her. "Come on, Miles."

"Mom said it's important for us to give Uncle Hal his privacy," Lilith said, marching along beside me.

"I thought you just said he wasn't home. How can I disturb him if he isn't back yet?"

"The mindful warrior does not stir the wasps' nest," Lilith said, but she'd stopped following me.

"We're just going to check to see if he's in his room, Lilith — that's all," I said, marching onto the porch. "We won't bother any wasps."

"Your sister's quoting Richard Harker," Miles said. "He's one of my heroes."

"You need to find a new hero, Miles," I said, going through the front door and starting down the hall to the kitchen.

"Hold on," he said, suddenly stopping. "The guy out front ... the one who helped me up ... that was ... that was Johnny Harker! Oh my God! That was Johnny Harker, wasn't it? Damn it, Charlie, your last name isn't Autumn, it's Harker! Am I right? I'm right, right?"

"That's what it says on my birth certificate," I said.

Upstairs, Jake and his men were busy hammering away at something.

"That means your father is Richard Harker," he said, his face lighting up.

"Nothing gets by you, Miles."

"That's incredible! I'm a huge fan! Is he coming here? Would he sign a copy of his books for me? When do you think he'll get here? He's coming, right?"

"If he ever gets here, and there's probably no chance of that happening, I'll make sure he signs all your books. Now, can we move along and check on Hal?"

"Sure, sure," he said, nodding and starting toward the kitchen. "You don't suppose Johnny would give me an autograph, do you?"

"I'll get the whole family to give you autographs when we're done," I said, heading through the kitchen and across to the pantry door.

"Richard Harker! This is incredible," Miles mumbled. "But wait — why does your mom go by Autumn? She kept her last name, is that it? My mom changed hers back when Dad died ..."

"Another mystery to add to your files," I said, and knocked. "Hello? Uncle Hal?"

I stopped and listened, but there was no answer. "Uncle Hal! Uncle Hal!" I cried and then turned to Miles. "He's kind of deaf."

"I observed that last night."

I pounded on the door. Still no answer.

"I guess Lilith was right. Looks like he's not back."

Miles reached by me, turned the doorknob and pushed the door open slowly.

A part of me, a large part of me, was expecting to find Hal sitting in the middle of a room wallpapered with tinfoil, aiming his shotgun at us. Instead, I was staring into a pantry absolutely stuffed with canned food. There were cans of peas, corn, peaches, pears, beans, chili, Spam and ham. There was tuna, salmon, sardines, shrimp, tomatoes, tomato paste, tomato sauce, diced tomatoes, ravioli, spaghetti, coconut milk, powdered milk, powdered eggs and even cans of whole chickens. Cans of everything you could imagine were jammed onto shelves on either side of the room, which was basically just a long, narrow closet. And at the end of it was another door.

"I'd say he prefers canned food to fresh or frozen," I said.

"Yeah, it looks like he's stocking up," Miles said.

"For what?" I asked, stepping over to the door at the back.

"Nuclear war, super flu, alien invasion ..."

"Are you sure you want to disturb a man who's stocking up for an alien invasion?" I asked, holding my hand up to the door.

"You didn't see what I saw last night. Something dangerous is happening in Rolling Hills, and we have to find out if he's been in —" He stopped suddenly and glanced at the floor, then looked back up. "Well, I need to know if he's all right."

"Uncle Hal?" I called, knocking. "Uncle Hal, it's me, Charlie. Are you in there?"

I knocked again, but there was no answer.

I tried the door. Surprisingly, it was unlocked, too. Hal didn't seem like the kind of man to leave his door unlocked, and I immediately got nervous. I had a vision of Hal crouching inside, surrounded by an army of antique dolls. But the door opened into an almost completely empty room.

"Looks like he moved out," I said.

Miles squeezed past me and went inside. It wasn't a big room. There was a cot in the corner, with a mattress still on it, but no sheets. There was a nightstand beside the cot. Miles rushed over to the cot and looked underneath it.

"Nothing," he grumbled, standing up and yanking open the drawer on the nightstand. I guess he didn't find anything in there either because he slammed it shut. There was another door in the far corner of the room, and that's where he headed next.

"What's in here?" he asked.

"Probably a portal to another dimension?"

Miles knocked on the door. "Mr. Autumn, are you in there?"

"Uncle Hal!" I yelled. "It's me! Charlie! We're going to open this door! Don't shoot!"

There was no answer, so Miles eased the door open and peered inside. I took a step back.

"Just a bathroom," he said, and marched back into the middle of the room. "This doesn't make any sense. I thought you said he was living in here."

"That's what my mom said, but who knows."

"Maybe he's set up camp in the woods," Miles said. "It would explain why we haven't seen him since last night."

"Yeah, maybe, but why would he have a lifetime's supply of canned food stuffed in the pantry if he was living out in the woods? That doesn't seem normal, does it?"

Miles was about to answer when Mom marched in, making my heart actually stop beating for about three seconds.

"What are you two doing in here?"

"You shouldn't sneak up on people like that," I said, pounding on my chest to get my heart started again. "Especially when they're busy snooping around in a crazy man's room."

"I thought I told you to respect Hal's privacy," she said.

"Aren't you concerned about your brother's welfare?" I asked. "Your *only* brother's welfare? I hate to break it to you, Mom, but he may have disappeared."

"He hasn't disappeared just because he's not in his room."

"There's nothing in his room," I said. "Isn't that strange?"

"When it comes to Hal, that's only a little strange."

"He might be hurt," Miles said.

"Thank you for your concern, Miles," she said, "but unless you'd like to pitch in and start scraping paint, I'm going to have to ask you to come back another time."

"I'd be happy to help," Miles said.

"Oh man, that's a huge mistake," I said.

"I can't pay you anything," Mom added.

"That's fine, Ms. Autumn. I love manual labor. Plus, maybe this will make up for the way I disturbed you last night."

Mom sighed. "I think we have an extra scraper in the truck."

"You're not seriously going to spend your day scraping paint?" I said, trudging back into the kitchen behind Miles.

"It'll give me a chance to see if Hal comes back," he whispered. "I need to know."

Saturday, 4:05 p.m.

We spent the rest of the afternoon scraping paint off the exterior of the inn, and I felt like a huge wad of Jell-O when Mom finally called us in at four o'clock. There was a cooler, stuffed with bottles of soda and ice, sitting just inside the kitchen door. Johnny and I each grabbed a bottle, Lilith declined (adding that she'd never contaminate herself with that junk) and Miles stood in the doorway.

"Charlie, did you put on any sunscreen today?" Mom asked.

"A smidge," I said, opening the soda and chugging back half the bottle.

"When?"

"About six hours ago," I said and burped loudly.

"You should have reapplied," she said, frowning. "You look like a boiled lobster."

"I feel like one, too," I said, and finished off the rest of my drink. "Maybe I should take the day off tomorrow. You know, just to make sure the skin peels off evenly."

"We talked about this, Charlie. We can't afford to have you take a whole day off."

"Have you seen Mr. Autumn yet?" Miles asked, cutting in.

"I'm afraid not," Mom said. "Help yourself to a drink, Miles. You did a lot of work today."

"Thank you, but I have to get going," he said. "However, if you don't mind, I'd like to drop by later this evening."

"Just make sure it's before nine, okay? I'm beat."

"Sure," he said. "And thanks for the autograph, Johnny."

"*De nada*," Johnny said, and Miles left.

"Is the shower finished?" Lilith asked.

"The plumber was sick today. We're hoping to have it fixed by tomorrow."

"Oh snap, Ma," Johnny said. "I totally reek, and I've got a date tonight."

"A date?" I said. "How did you line up a date? You

haven't been here for twenty-four hours, and you've spent most of thc time blasting paint off of the side of the inn."

"I got a text from Elizabeth," he said, shrugging.

"That reminds me," I said, turning to Mom. "I need a new phone."

"I told you, Charlie, I'm not buying you a new phone. You've got your computer and your tablet. You don't need another phone to lose."

"I can't walk around with a tablet in my pocket, Mom. And during my long and arduous walk home today, I was thinking that I should probably have a phone in case I get into some kind of trouble or get lost. I mean, what if there's an emergency?"

"It's a small town, Charlie. The people are friendly. I'm sure you'll manage," she said.

"What about the shower situation?" Johnny asked.

"Go down to the river. There's a place called The Bend where I used to go swimming. Take the truck."

"Look," I said, "bathing in the river is all well and good for the television star of the family. Apparently he can line up dates standing on the side of the road in the middle of the night, but how am I supposed to meet anyone if I'm walking around in Choke clothes and smell like a mix of BO and dirty river water? I say we book into a hotel while we wait for this place to get fixed up."

"First, Charlie, the river's not dirty," Mom said. "And second, the bathroom will be done by tomorrow. There's no reason for us to leave."

"Not yet, anyway," I said. "Not yet."

Saturday, 4:40 p.m.

Lilith stayed behind with Mom while Johnny and I piled into the truck and headed down to the river. I'd been picturing a private little watering hole, with birds singing in the trees and fish swimming around us. Instead, the road was lined with cars, and The Bend was absolutely packed with people.

It wasn't hard to figure out why it was called The Bend — it was just a long curve in the Rolling River that would look like a giant *C* from above. The inside part of the *C* consisted of a smoothed-down, solid ledge of rock that gradually sloped down from the woods behind it into the water. The ledge was covered with people, lying on towels. We were standing on the road, on the outer edge of the *C*, looking down on them. On the other side of the guardrail was a high cliff that dropped straight into the river. A gang of kids was standing on the edge and taking turns leaping into the air and screaming their way down into the water. The river was about as wide as the road, and there was a mix of people floating around on air mattresses, inner tubes or just swimming lazily in the black water.

Up the river and to our left, there was a wooden bridge that you could cross to get to the rock ledge on the other side. Johnny headed for the bridge, but I was feeling lazy, so I got in line with the ten-year-olds on the edge of the cliff. When it was my turn, I kicked off my flip-flops and took a flying leap into the water.

I'm not sure if my sunburn was a factor, but the water was like ice, and I think I had a minor heart attack when I went under. It was pitch-black down there, and the water got colder and colder the deeper I went. By the time I came back up, I was gasping for air and quickly turning from red to blue.

"Are you all right?" a kid on an inner tube asked, paddling over.

"I'll be fine, as soon as my heart starts up again," I said, breaststroking my way toward the ledge on the inside of the *C*.

Five feet from the water's edge, I could stand up on the part of the rock shelf that extended into the water. I eased my way up onto dry ground and lay down to bask in the sun.

"Nice entry, bro," Johnny said, sitting down beside me.

"Thanks, I'm in training for the next Olympics."

"Oh yeah? For what event?"

"The Jumping-Into-Ice-Cold-Water event. How did I look?"

"Fearless," he said.

That's when I heard someone behind us say, "Isn't that Jaysin Night?"

"I think you've been spotted."

"I think you're right," he said, as people started murmuring behind us.

"By the way, the water's just a smidgen on the chilly side."

"Thanks for the warning, bro," he said and yanked his shirt off. Johnny's ripped, of course, and I heard the murmuring behind us get a little more frantic.

"Hop along there, Cassidy, or they're going to get to you before you can get into the water and wash off all your Hollywood BO."

Johnny marched into the river, dove under and came up on the other side, grinning.

"That is most definitely Jaysin Night," someone said behind me.

"Are you sure?"

"I'd recognize that body anywhere. What's his real name?"

"I don't know."

"I think it's Jack."

A second later, four girls in bikinis padded by me and slipped into the water.

"Hi!" one of them called as they swam out to meet Johnny.

"Hi," Johnny said, and they giggled a little.

Interrupting them now would be bad form, so I lay back, closed my eyes and was drifting off when someone sat down beside me.

"That must get annoying."

I opened my eyes a crack and saw Elizabeth Opal sitting next to me. Her long red hair was tied back in a ponytail, and she was wearing a black bikini.

"Nah, not really," I said, springing up and into a sitting position. "Even before Johnny was a big star, he had gaggles of girls following him around. I really wouldn't bother with him if I were you. I'm sure there are far more interesting people to get to know."

"They're behaving like idiots," she said as the girls all giggled again.

"They're not your friends?"

"Not really," she said. "I grew up in Rolling Hills, but

I don't go to school here, so I always feel like a bit of an outsider."

"Where do you go to school?"

"Winehurst Girls' Academy, but my dad almost sent me to Choke," she said, nodding at my T-shirt, which I hadn't bothered to take off.

"Winehurst is a fine institution."

"I suppose," she said, looking out at Johnny, who was now sitting near the edge of the water, saying something that was making all the girls laugh harder. "Most of the people there are snobs, and I hate the uniforms." She glanced back at me. "I guess you don't mind yours."

"Sure, I love gallivanting around in my uniform! Heck, I wanted to go swimming in my full uniform — blazer and tie. But my mom wouldn't allow it. She said it would be too pretentious. What do you think?"

"I think you're crazy."

"Or a fashionable trendsetter."

"Hmm. Or maybe you got too much sun today."

"Are you saying that sunburns aren't in style in Rolling Hills? They're all the rage at Choke."

"Are you always so sarcastic?"

"Only when I'm talking to the most beautiful girl in town."

"See," she said, "now I know you're just being sarcastic. Do you take anything seriously?"

Johnny had left his harem of starstruck fans behind, and he sat down beside Elizabeth.

"You didn't tell me Charlie was so funny," she said to him.

"He never quits," Johnny said, grinning.

"I don't think those girls are going to quit either," I said, nodding at his fans, who were getting out of the water, too.

"Yeah," he said, "I guess we're going to have to come here when it's not so busy."

"Wait until July, when the tourists arrive. You won't be able to find a square inch of space to sit down in," Elizabeth said.

"And when they find out that Jaysin Night enjoys the occasional midnight skinny-dip, they'll have to sell tickets to this place," I added.

"Come on, bro. Cut me some slack."

"He's right, though. Maybe not about the skinny-dips — I wouldn't know about that ..." Elizabeth said, blushing a little. "But you're big news, Johnny. And I think they're going to want a few pictures." She nodded toward the girls, who were now coming our way with their phones.

"Time for me to go," I said.

"Me, too," Elizabeth added, and we both got up. "Are we still on for tonight, Johnny?"

"You bet," he said.

"I'll meet you at The Opal at eight. Bring an appetite."

"Will do," he said. "Why don't you stick around, bro. I can give you a lift back."

"No, I've been in enough pictures with you, Johnny. I'll walk back to the inn. It'll help me thaw out."

That's when the mob arrived. It included the four girls,

with phones, and about seven other people who had recognized Johnny. They jostled around, trying to get a picture with him, while I wandered away with Elizabeth.

We crossed the bridge and looked back down at The Bend. The crowd had gotten bigger, and Johnny was busy being a good sport and smiling for the cameras.

"What's he really like?" she asked.

My heart sank. It was a question that a hundred girls had asked me over the years. I had been hoping Elizabeth was going to be different.

I was about to answer when she laughed. "I'm kidding, Charlie. That's got to be the single dumbest question I could possibly ask."

"Beautiful, smart *and* funny," I said, shaking my head. "You're a triple threat, Winehurst."

She laughed. "Do you want a drive home?"

"No, I think I could use a little more sun. Plus, Johnny will find a way to escape from his groupies in a few minutes."

"Suit yourself," she said, smiling. "I'll see you later, Charlie."

"Later, Winehurst," I said. Then I watched her walk back to her Porsche and drive away for the second time that day. I didn't actually think Johnny would be done with his fans in a few minutes, but Elizabeth was clearly more interested in Johnny, and I really didn't want to compete for her attention. I've learned you can't play that game against Johnny Harker and come out on top.

Saturday, 5:45 p.m.

Instead of milling around by the river, I decided to start walking back to the inn. I figured Johnny might get caught up posing for photos for ten minutes, but ten minutes came and went, and there was still no sign of him. Twenty minutes passed, and then thirty, and every time I heard the sound of an engine coming down Elm Street my heart did a little dance (my feet were too tired to dance). Two cars passed me, but neither was a giant black pickup truck with a television star behind the wheel. The second one was a Jeep filled with local yokels about my age. The guy in the passenger seat gave me the finger on the way by, proof that Rolling Hills was a normal enough kind of place after all. I thanked him for his kindness and continued to trudge along the gravel shoulder. Thankfully, the trees were tall enough to keep me in the shade, because it was still stinking hot outside, and my sunburn was starting to irritate me. After forty minutes with just the sound of my feet scuffling along, I was lulled into a partially hypnotic state. I have no doubt I would have wandered by the Baxter place without even knowing it if Miles Van Helsing hadn't snapped me out of my trance.

"Psst," he hissed.

"Huh?" I said, looking around.

"In here," he said, and a hand reached out of a nearby bush and dragged me off the gravel shoulder.

Miles was still dressed in black, only he had his baseball cap on backward and a pair of binoculars around his neck.

"The Baxter residence," he said, pointing behind me.

I turned and saw a two-story house at the top of a low hill across the street. It was an old country house, but well cared for, painted white with green trim. There was a porch out front with four green wooden deck chairs, two on each side of the front door, which was also painted green. The lawn was immaculate and there was a green mailbox at the bottom of the driveway with *The Baxters* painted along the side.

"That's where the monsters live?" I asked.

"Creepy, isn't it?" Miles said, in not much more than a whisper.

"No, Miles, it's not creepy. It's ridiculously normal."

"That's why it's so creepy."

"I can't believe I nearly fell for all this," I said, and started back for the road, but as I was walking away, a man came out the front door. He was wearing a straw fedora, sunglasses, a long-sleeve blue dress shirt and khaki pants. He looked about as average as average can get.

"Baxter," Miles hissed, pulling me back behind the bushes.

Baxter walked to a black Volvo parked beside the house, got in, started it up and backed down the driveway. He pulled onto Elm Street, stopping for a moment to switch the car from reverse into drive. He was only a few yards away from us, and I got a pretty good look at him. I didn't notice any glowing red eyes or fangs, and he wasn't moving with jerky spasms. He was just an average Joe going for a drive. I watched him for a moment, and then he drove away.

"I'm leaving, Miles — and you should, too. Go back

home, blog about your paranoid conspiracy theories and then have a nap. You need to clear the cobwebs out of your brain."

"You can't go that way," he said, grabbing my arm. "You'll blow my cover."

"There's no cover to blow, Miles. People around here already know you're certifiable," I said, yanking my arm free. "Plus, Baxter just left — or did you miss that?"

I was just about to step out onto the gravel shoulder when he grabbed me from behind. "*Mrs.* Baxter is still inside," he hissed.

That's when Johnny finally drove by in the truck.

"My ride!" I barked, struggling out of his hold. "I just missed my ride, you nut-bar!"

"Oh, sorry, Charlie ... Uh ... why don't you borrow mine?" he said. "It's just up this way."

I almost turned down the offer out of pure frustration, but my feet wouldn't budge, and my sunburn was starting to throb nicely.

"Fine," I said.

Miles smiled. "Follow me."

We walked for about a hundred yards through the woods before he cut up toward the street and arrived at his minicycle, which was propped against a tree a few feet off the road.

"This is Shelley," he said, wheeling it toward the road. "I built her myself."

"Out of what?" I asked, glancing at the black tubing that wound its way into the shape of a frame and surrounded a block of an engine.

"I pieced her together, using parts from this and that. Bring it to the Voodoo tonight. I'll be waiting," he said, wheeling it onto the side of Elm Street. "Do you know how to drive a motorcycle?"

"Sure," I said, hopping on. I might not have my driver's license, but that didn't mean I hadn't had the opportunity to ride a few motorcycles in my time. I'm not saying that's a smart thing to do — it's not. In fact, all three times I'd driven a motorcycle I'd just about killed myself, but you can only travel around the world so many times with your family before someone, somewhere, asks if you'd like to hop on their ride.

I got on and started up the engine. It gave a chugging roar.

"Go easy. It's got a little more juice than you think," Miles said, and darted back into the trees.

I kind of jerked my way down the road at first but got comfortable pretty fast and upped the speed. Miles wasn't lying; it definitely had some kick, and by the time I got back to the inn I was buzzing along nicely, the breeze soothing my sunburn. I didn't really want to slow down and I would have barreled into the driveway except I remembered what had happened to Miles. So, I let up on the throttle and rolled cautiously into the driveway, not much above a jogging pace.

Mom, Lilith and Johnny were all sitting on the porch, eating pizza. When Mom spotted me, her expression hardened, and she leaped out of her chair.

"What the heck do you think you're doing driving that thing without a helmet?" she yelled.

"It was only a couple of minutes, Mom, and in case you didn't notice, it's not a long fall off of one of these things," I said, slowly riding the bike down the gravel walkway and right up to the porch steps. "I wouldn't have had to use it in the first place if Johnny hadn't abandoned me."

"Don't go there, bro," Johnny said. "You were the one who abandoned me. I was stuck signing autographs for almost an hour."

"My heart bleeds for you," I said, stepping onto the porch.

There were two pizza boxes sitting on the floor. I opened the first one, but there was no cheese on it.

"Life's too short to eat pizza without cheese, Lilith," I said.

"Life is empty with no standards, Charlie," she said.

"Is that one of Dad's famous sayings?" I said, grabbing a slice from the other box. Not only did it have cheese — lots of it — but it had pepperoni, too.

"You really need to read his books," she grumbled.

"You don't ride that thing ever again — do you understand me, Charlie?" Mom barked.

"Cross my heart and hope to die," I said and ripped into the pizza.

Mom let it drop, and we ended up sitting around on the porch, eating pizza and chatting. It was nice not to have to rush anywhere or do anything. It felt like the first time in a very long time that we all just sat around without a care in the world.

"Now this is what summer is supposed to be like," I said. "Why don't we take a break from the scraping, just for a few days ... for the weekend, at least? I'm sure Jake and his boys can handle it."

"You know we can't do that, Charlie," Mom said.

"Nice try, bro," Johnny said, standing up. "And it's been a blast, but I've got to get changed for dinner."

"Didn't we just eat dinner?" I asked, holding up a half-finished slice of pizza.

"I'm bulking up, bro," he said, heading for the front door. "Are you still taking me into town, Ma? Elizabeth said my flat tire's fixed."

"Sure, I'd like to go and grab some ice cream," she said, getting up, too. "Who's with me?"

"Can I rub it on my skin?" I asked. The sunburn was really starting to sting now.

"You deserve that burn," Lilith said. "It's not a joke anymore, is it?"

"Don't be so sure, Lilypad. In a week, when my skin is done peeling away, we'll have a good laugh about the day Charlie got scorched. You wait and see."

"Unless you get skin cancer."

"What a wonderful outlook you have," I said, but I don't think she heard me because they'd all gone inside.

Saturday, 7:40 p.m.

By the time I'd eased my sore skin into a wrinkly pair of khakis and a not-quite-clean, plain white T-shirt, the sun was starting to dip beneath the trees. Mom had cajoled Lilith into joining us, even though she didn't eat ice cream thanks to her wacky vegan diet. She also insisted I return

Miles's minicycle ASAP, and I told her I thought we could bring it to a place on Church Street where he hung out. So, we loaded it into the back of the pickup and headed for downtown Rolling Hills.

We dropped Johnny off at the garage, so he could pick up his precious motorcycle, and then turned onto Church Street, which was hopping. Cars were cruising up and down the street, folks were wandering along the sidewalk, popping in and out of stores. Lots of people were just standing around, chatting or sipping sodas or coffee. We couldn't even find a parking spot until we were past The Opal, which was okay by me because it put us closer to the Voodoo Juice Bar.

We hoisted the minicycle onto the sidewalk, and a group of about ten girls, all around my age, wandered past and down the alley toward the Voodoo.

"I'm going to drop this off to Miles," I said. "I'll meet you back at the inn."

"Don't you want some ice cream?" Mom asked.

"I'll take a rain check," I said, starting toward the alley.

"I thought you said the walk home was too hard from down here," Lilith added.

"It's not that hot anymore now that the sun is a little lower," I said without turning around. Which was true; it wasn't nearly as hot as it had been that morning, although my burn wasn't exactly cooling me down.

"Don't be too late," Mom called as I wheeled the bike into the alley.

I heard the Voodoo before I saw it. Some kind of electronic music that sounded like it was made by a deranged robot was wafting down the alley. I propped Miles's bike against the wall outside and went in. The place was packed. I recognized a few faces from The Bend that afternoon. Apparently a few of them recognized me, too, because as soon as I started for the bar a group of three girls ran up to me.

"Oh my God! Is Jaysin Night going to be here?" one of them asked. She was short, with shoulder-length brown hair and big brown eyes.

"Unfortunately, he has to do battle with a pack of vampires in another small town," I said.

"Oh no, really?" she said, her shoulders slumping.

"But hey, I'm his brother, Charlie. Why don't we grab a seat, you could buy me a Re-Animator and I could tell you all about him."

I think they were about to take me up on my offer when Miles Van Helsing stormed between us and grabbed me by the shoulders.

"Thank God you're here. I could really use your help."

He was wearing the same black clothes as before, only now he had a black backpack strapped on.

"Miles, you're seriously cramping my style. I was just about to sit down with these lovely ladies and enjoy a delicious Re-Animator."

"What? Who?" he said, and seemed to notice for the first time that I'd actually been talking to someone. "Well, can't you do that later? I need your help."

"It'll have to wait," I said and tried to shuffle by him, but it was too late. The girls were already walking away.

"Did your uncle Hal get back?"

"No," I said, watching the girls sit down in the corner. "Your Harley's out in the alley, by the way."

"Her name is Shelley, not Harley," he said. "Why don't you buy yourself a drink and meet me outside in five minutes."

"I don't ..." I started, but he was already heading for the door.

I ordered my drink from Vortex, who was still wearing a white lab coat. A minute or two later, he handed me a Re-Animator in one hand and a note in the other.

"What's this?" I asked.

He didn't answer, but just walked away and took another drink order.

I took a sip of the Re-Animator and was pleasantly surprised to find it tasted even better than the one I'd had that morning. Then I opened the note. It read: **Notice anything strange?**

I hadn't noticed anything strange, and part of me didn't want to humor the man by looking around. I was already too caught up with Miles; I didn't need Vortex making me edgy, too. But it's hard to get a note that says, **Notice anything strange?**, and not look around, so I did.

At first I was relieved, because I didn't see anything out of the ordinary. I took another sip of the Re-Animator and scanned the room for the girl with the big brown eyes. That's when I noticed three guys standing in the far corner, all with jackets on, hoods up and still wearing their sunglasses despite the fact that the Voodoo was a pretty shadowy place to begin with. It wasn't just the hoods and the sunglasses, though. What really got me was the way they were standing — stock-still against the wall, with a look of utter boredom on their faces. No, it wasn't boredom; it was a wooden, completely emotionless look. The kind of look the bodyguards you see surrounding important politicians have — you know they're watching, but they look like they couldn't care less about anything that's going on around them. You could almost have taken them for a bunch of mannequins, but even in the semi-darkness of the Voodoo I could tell they were real people. I didn't like admitting it, but Dr. Vortex was right — they were strange, and not in a good way. That's when Miles came back in.

"Let's go," he said. "I'm going to get some proof — some video evidence — and post it online. But I need help. I need *your* help, Charlie."

"Why me?" I said, thinking that, despite the creepy mannequin gang, I'd still rather go sit down with the girl with the big brown eyes.

"I can't drive and record those things at the same time."

"It'll have to wait," I said, and started toward the brown-eyed girl's table.

"No, no, no," Miles said, scampering beside me. "This *can't* wait. I have a working hypothesis that after sundown, those who have been ... um ... well, changed ... become physically stronger somehow. I think it has something to do with UV rays. So, it's imperative that we're present before and after the sun sets."

"Look," I said, turning to face Miles, a few feet from the girls' table. "During summer vacation, I like to sleep in, relax, maybe make a few friends, like the fine individuals sitting behind me. What I *don't* like to do is invade people's privacy by secretly recording them with the town lunatic while they change into some kind of imaginary paranormal whatever."

"So, you admit that people are changing into something."

"I believe, wholeheartedly, that *you* believe people are changing into something. But that does not mean there is a *we*, Miles. *You* believe people are changing, and *I* believe I'd like to sit down and meet the girl with the lovely brown eyes sitting behind me."

"There's nobody sitting behind you."

I turned. The brown-eyed girl was gone, along with her friends.

"I could really use your help," Miles said.

I glanced around the room. It was no good. They were really gone. And the three mannequins that had been standing by the wall were gone, too.

I threw back the rest of the Re-Animator and slammed the jar down on the bar.

"The three guys with the sunglasses — what happened to them?" I asked, pointing at the back wall.

"They left."

"When?"

"At the same time as the girls. Right around the time you were telling me about what you like to do during your summer vacations."

I rushed across the room and out into the alley. It was empty. The sun wasn't down yet, but the light was fading.

I ran around the corner and back out to Church Street.

It was still busy; I couldn't spot the girls or the three mannequins. A moment later, Miles ran up beside me.

"How could you just let them walk out like that, with those three guys hanging around?" I snapped.

"They didn't leave together — not exactly."

"They were obviously ..." I started and then hesitated. "They were clearly ... well, they seemed a little odd."

"Yes, they were odd," Miles said seriously. "Something bad is happening, Charlie. This is my hometown. I know these people," he said, gesturing toward the street with his hands, "and I don't want them to get infected."

"Infected?"

"It's just a hypothesis," he said. "We have to test it first, and then show the evidence to the world. We need to move, Charlie, or it's going to be too late."

I took one last look along Church Street for the girl with the brown eyes or the mannequin triplets. I didn't see any of them.

"Fine," I said, "but I want the record to show that the only reason I'm doing this is because I'm lazy and don't want to walk all the way back to the inn."

"Done!" he said.

Saturday, 8:30 p.m.

Miles led me back down the alley, past the Voodoo and a couple of stores, and over to a collection of garbage bins that smelled like coffee grounds. His minicycle was parked just beyond the garbage cans, but now there was a red wagon attached to the back.

"What's the wagon for?" I asked.

"For you," he said, sliding his backpack off. He unzipped it and pulled out a small handheld video camera. "You need to record what we see."

"Are you sure Shelley has enough juice to pull me?" I said, taking the camera.

"I've made some adjustments to the engine," he said, putting on the backpack. "It'll do the job."

"This thing isn't going to fall off halfway up one of those hills?" I asked, climbing into the wagon.

"Not a chance," he said, starting up the bike and sliding on a dark green helmet that looked like it was issued by the military in about 1943. There were old-style goggles wrapped around the helmet, which he slid down over his eyes.

"Shouldn't I be wearing a helmet, too?" I asked, but Miles just revved the engine and tore off down the alley.

I jangled along, gripping the sides of the wagon as we hurtled by garbage bins and the rear doors of the shops that lined Church Street. We were driving away from Oak Avenue, toward the other end of Church, and I could see the end of the alley speeding toward us when one of the rear doors flew open and a man wearing a white apron stepped in front of us. I would have screamed, but I didn't have time. Miles swerved toward the brick wall on our right, missed a collection of garbage bins by the width of my fingernails and torpedoed past the man.

"Stupid idiot!" the man roared.

A half second later, Miles whizzed out of the alley and onto Maple Drive without slowing down. We careened off of the curb, and I was sure the wagon would split apart, but it held, and Miles scooted into the middle of the road. A minivan was about 2.3 seconds from hitting us, and the driver laid on the horn, but Miles managed to pull a shockingly quick turn back to our side of the street, with me and the wagon skidding along sideways behind him.

"Moron!" the driver hollered as he drove by, shaking a fist at us.

"It's clear sailing from here on," Miles shouted back to me, apparently unconcerned by the fact that we'd almost been killed twice in the last thirty seconds.

Saturday, 8:45 p.m.

Maple was lined with two-story houses with large lawns, most of which were surrounded by white picket fences. Occasionally, there'd be someone out front, chatting with a neighbor or doing some yard work, and they'd stop what they were doing as we approached, the lunatic screech of the engine preceding us. I waved at a few of the gawkers, but I mostly just held on to the sides of the wagon for dear life, bouncing along with the camera in my lap. At the top of Maple, we came to a T-junction with Elm Street and took a right, heading back toward the inn. Seven or eight minutes later we drove past the Baxter place. About fifty yards beyond their driveway, Miles pulled over.

"Just made it," he said, cutting the engine and hopping off the bike.

He was right: the thinnest slivers of red sunlight were glinting through the trees.

"Now what?" I asked, getting out of the wagon.

"Now we sneak around back and catch them in the act," he said, leaving his helmet on.

"The act of what?"

"I'm not sure," he said. "But we'll know it when we see it."

"That's very scientific, Miles."

"This will provide us with an excellent opportunity to film them while they're moving."

"What do you mean 'moving'?"

"When they're pursuing us," he said.

"That doesn't sound like a good plan, Miles, not good at all. I mean, don't get me wrong, I have a feeling we're just going to end up with a couple of angry, middle-aged people on our hands, but if they are something else and they can move as fast as you say, then that's not a solid plan at all."

"Don't worry, Charlie, my bike can move pretty fast. You just make sure you keep filming. Is the camera on?"

"Sure," I said, pressing Record and aiming it at Miles.

He straightened up, flipped his goggles up onto the helmet and looked directly into the camera. "This is Miles Van Helsing, June twenty-fourth," he started, then glanced at his watch, "at 8:47 p.m. I'm about to investigate the Baxter residence for signs of paranormal activity and the presence of unknown humanoid creatures. Assisting me will be Charles Harker, who is behind the camera."

"Good luck, Van Helsing!" I cried.

He grimaced and ducked a little. "Keep it down."

"Good luck, Van Helsing," I whispered.

"Just keep the camera rolling," he said and jogged up the driveway, his backpack bouncing up and down behind him. I turned the camera around and held it out at arm's length.

"This is Charles Richard Harker, on June twenty-something at a quarter past a mole. I'm currently standing at the bottom of the Baxters' driveway. Miles Van Helsing, a Grade A nut-job, is here searching for people who can run very fast. I suggested he'd have more luck at the local running track, but he insisted on inspecting his neighbor's house for signs of abnormally quick individuals. I, for one, hope he finds what he's been looking for so that I can go home and go to sleep. Over and under, Charles Richard Harker."

I lowered the camera and took a look around. The sun was almost gone now, and the trees that lined the Baxters' driveway were sending long black shadows across the pavement. The Volvo was back, parked at the top of the driveway beside the house, but all the windows were shut and the curtains were all closed. There wasn't a single light on inside. It made me think that the Baxters were probably out, maybe taking a long walk, which would be good news because it meant that Miles would be done here soon. Then I could go home and laze around until I fell asleep. A solid night's sleep would be sweet. Tomorrow, if we went back to Romero's for breakfast, I'd hop down to the Voodoo and ask Vortex if he knew the brown-eyed girl's name. Then, who knows? Maybe I could track down her phone number. That's what I was thinking about as I meandered up the driveway, listening to a crow cawing somewhere close by. Other than that, the evening was silent. It was silent, that is, until I heard a small, short scream that made me freeze. The crow flapped away, and a second later, Miles sprinted around the back corner of the house. I say he was sprinting, but it was more than just sprinting; he was practically falling the whole way down the driveway, his mouth wide open, like he was about to scream.

"Run!" he barked, eyes bulging out of his head.

Before I had a chance to react, three people came around the same corner of the house. They were running in single file, which I had to admit looked pretty creepy after all. They were moving incredibly fast — faster than I've ever seen anybody move in my life. Faster than Miles, and it looked like he was about to start flying. Despite how quickly they were sprinting, their faces looked completely blank, like they were sitting on the couch watching paint dry. Baxter was leading the way, wearing the same blue dress shirt and the same khaki pants that I'd seen him in earlier. The man behind him was a big bear of a man, with short black hair and wearing a navy blue suit. The last one was a woman wearing jeans and a white blouse.

"Run, Charlie!" Miles screamed, racing past me.

I turned and tore into the road right behind him, still holding the camera.

"Hurry!" Miles cried, glancing over his shoulder. His

eyebrows were so high on his forehead they were practically touching his hairline. "Hurry!"

Miles reached the minicycle, started it up and pulled away when I was still five or six feet from the wagon. That's when I made the mistake of peeking over my shoulder. The three of them were only about ten feet behind me. Panicked, I dove for the wagon and landed with a thud in the middle of it, my legs hanging out the back. The bike and wagon wobbled dangerously to the left and then the right, and I thought Miles was going to wipe out, but he managed to straighten up. Unfortunately, all that wobbling cost us speed, and Baxter was suddenly running right beside me.

He looked down, his face still completely blank but turning a deep crimson. He was running at a tremendous speed, a ridiculous speed, and beads of sweat were pouring down his head and into his eyes. He reached for me.

I dropped the camera, which clattered into the wagon, and batted his hand away. He stumbled, lost some speed and then caught up again.

"Faster!" I yelled, and Miles must have changed gears because we shot forward.

Baxter fell back again, but another hand grabbed the back of my shirt, this time from the other side of the wagon. I was being lifted up and turned to see the Man-Bear in the navy blue suit. He was hoisting me out of the wagon with one hand.

"Miles!" I yelled, grabbing on to the sides of the wagon. "Faster!"

Miles glanced back, his mouth dropped open and he revved the engine until it sounded like a whistle that was about to explode. We picked up more speed, and Man-Bear fell back a little, but he didn't let go of my shirt. He was pulling me out, and my hands slipped along the sides of the wagon. I looked up at his face, where a vein had popped out in the middle of his huge forehead. Up until now his mouth had been shut, but now he opened it wide and sucked in air. That's when I saw his teeth. There were normal teeth in his mouth, but there were other teeth in there, too, slipping out of his gums. They were scattered here and there, white and sharp, like thick pins. He started pulling me back harder and at the same time lowered his head toward me, his mouth wide. He was going to try to bite me!

One of the things I like least in life is being bitten, so I snatched up the video camera and chucked it at Man-Bear's face. It hit his right eye and bounced away. His mouth snapped shut, but he held on to me for another second, his expression staying absolutely empty despite being corked in the face with the camera. Then blood poured out from a cut just under his eyebrow and he let go. I fell back into the wagon and pitched to my left, which sent the wagon reeling onto two wheels. I rode it like that, sure that we were going to flip over, for what felt like three and a half hours before Miles veered to the right and the wheels crashed down.

This time I was sure the wagon would fall apart, but it held together again. I made a mental note to send a beautifully worded thank-you letter to whoever made that wagon, and Miles managed to pick up a little more speed. I looked back — the three of them had stopped chasing us and were standing in the middle of the road. They stared back at me as the shadowy twilight moved toward full dark.

Saturday, 8:58 p.m.

Miles didn't slow down until we were back at the inn. When he finally eased off the gas, Shelley chugged in fits and coughs into the middle of the driveway.

"I think I might've killed her," he said, getting off the minicycle.

"Better her than us," I said, jumping out of the wagon.

"You saw them, right?" he muttered, as we made a dash for the front door. "You saw them."

"I saw them," I stammered, glancing back at the road.

We ran onto the porch and I grabbed the doorknob, praying Mom had left it unlocked. She hadn't.

"We're out in the middle of nowhere. Why would she lock the doors?"

Miles didn't respond; he just crouched behind one of the rosebushes that lined the other side of the railing.

"Did you hear that?" he asked, his head cocked toward the trees, his eyes somehow growing even bigger, making him look like a terrified human-owl hybrid.

I hadn't heard anything, but I was so jacked up on adrenaline by that point, I wasn't sure any of my senses were working properly, so I hid beside him and we peeked out over the bush. The porch, the lawn, the driveway, the road, they were all empty.

"Where's the video camera?" Miles whispered, still peering into the night.

"Gone," I said.

"What do you mean?"

"I had to use it on the Man-Bear," I said. "Otherwise I'd be toast right now."

"But the recording! The proof!" he cried, standing up.

"Don't freak out," I said, pulling him down. "They probably just left it on the road."

"Don't freak out! On the road!" he said, standing up again. "Charlie, we need to get it!"

"No, we don't, Miles," I said, pulling him down again. "Not now, we don't."

"Nobody's going to believe us without some evidence. We need to show people what's going on around here, Charlie! You saw them — they were changed. We've got to get that camera!"

"You want to go out there again? You said it yourself — your minicycle's practically dead. Those people, whatever they are, will chase you down in three seconds flat."

"I don't care, Charlie," he said, slinking over to the porch stairs. "We need to warn people. We can't just sit in here and hide like a couple of chickens."

"What are we going to tell them, anyway?" I said, grabbing his arm. "I mean, what did we just see? Three people who were ridiculously fast and strong, who just happened to have pointy teeth sticking out of their gums?"

"Fangs?" Miles asked.

"I barely know what I saw anymore. I mean, I was

pretty amped up. It was dark — I was probably imagining things."

"No, no, that makes sense. It's the type of anatomical changes I would expect under the circumstances."

"What circumstances? Maybe they just have a bad case of rabies," I said. "Or they're hopped up on some drug."

"Rabies doesn't give you fangs, and it can't make you move that fast, and I don't think there are any drugs that would do that either."

"I'm pretty sure there are a few drugs you can buy to make you run faster."

"I'm not talking about steroids, Charlie. I was going close to thirty-five miles an hour, for Pete's sake."

"That's pretty fast."

"Pretty fast? After what I saw last night, I looked up how fast the best sprinters in the world can run. Do you know how fast they go?"

"Thirty-five miles an hour?"

"Around twenty-four miles an hour. That means the man in the blue suit was running eleven miles per hour faster than the fastest sprinters on the planet, and he was doing it while he was lifting you up with one hand. That's not human, and it's not rabies or drugs," he said. "Do you know what they were doing when I found them around back?"

"I don't think I want to know," I said.

"They were standing in Mr. Baxter's barn, in a triangle, staring at each other. They weren't talking — they were just standing and staring. That's classic hive-mind behavior."

"Okay, so what do you think we're dealing with?"

"I don't want to make any outlandish guesses, but I'd say we're definitely dealing with some kind of vampire- or zombie-like transmutation. Possibly even an extraterrestrial infection."

"Whoa, whoa there, hoss," I said. "Do you hear what you're saying? I don't think anyone's going to believe a vampire-zombie-alien transmoosomething theory, with or without video evidence. We've got a seriously messed-up situation on our hands — I'm with you on that — but I don't think we need to tell anyone that there are vampires running around Rolling Hills."

"Actually, I think their attributes are more closely associated with zombies," Miles said, looking thoughtful. "The blank looks on their faces, their jerky movements, the strange behavior, it's almost as though they're being driven beyond normal human limits by some other entity. It's like they're puppets. Perhaps it's a mind-control drug or a secret government implant of some sort?"

"Or maybe they're just good-old-fashioned crazy, Miles."

"Insanity is a possibility," he said, "but that wouldn't explain the fact that it seems to be spreading. I've never heard of insanity being passed from person to person."

"How do you know it's spreading?" I said, scanning the front yard for any signs of movement.

"Last night, when I first saw the Baxters, they were chasing the large man in the navy blue suit. Later on, and tonight, he was working with them. Plus, Dr. Vortex and I have noticed a few other people in town acting in a rather peculiar way. Even you noticed those guys at the Voodoo."

"Sure, but they might've just been antisocial."

"That's why you went running after them when they left?"

"Look, Miles, it doesn't matter if they're crazy, on drugs, or if they're vampires —"

"More like zombies," he said, cutting me off.

"Vampires, zombies — call them zompires for all I care!"

"Zompires? That's a ridiculous name."

"It doesn't matter! When my mom gets back, I'll tell her what happened, and we'll get the sheriff up here and he'll investigate. Then, we'll all check into a hotel about five hundred miles from here and forget about all this over a frosty lemonade by the pool."

"I couldn't run away like that, and I can't hide anymore, not with my camera out there somewhere," he said and peeked out at the front yard again.

"Don't be crazy," I said, taking a quick look myself. There was no sign of any movement; the leaves weren't even rustling in the breeze. The only noise was the crickets chirruping.

"Miles, don't be crazy," I said again, but he was already slinking down the porch steps.

"Don't!" I called, rushing after him.

Miles was already at the bottom when I heard the sound of a truck coming down the road. A few seconds later, the glow of headlights appeared, cutting through the night.

"It's my mom," I said, and then realized that the Baxters and Man-Bear could be lurking close by, ready to spring.

"We've got to warn them," Miles said, obviously thinking the same thing.

I bounded off the porch, and we sprinted across the lawn. We were about fifteen feet from the driveway when Mom pulled in and immediately ran over the wagon attached to Miles's minicycle. There was a popping crunch, and she backed up.

"What the devil was that?" she asked, bursting out of the truck.

"My wagon!" Miles cried, running over. "My wagon!"

"Why is that thing parked in my driveway?" she asked.

"Keep it down," I said, grabbing her elbow. "We need to go inside and call the sheriff."

"Why was there a wagon in the middle of my driveway?" she said, pulling her arm away. "Is the truck okay?"

"You don't understand," I said, glancing around. "We need to call the sheriff immediately. Miles was right — there *is* something weird going on in this town."

Lilith hopped out of the truck and kicked the tire that'd done the damage to the wagon. Then she squatted down and ran her hands over it.

"I think the truck is fine, Mom," she said, standing up.

"We've got to go inside," I said. "We've got to call the sheriff."

"Look, Charlie, I'm going to park this truck, then I'm going to go inside, put my feet up and relax. Then, and only then, will I permit you to explain to me what you're babbling about."

"Sure, sure," I said, grabbing her elbow again and hustling her back to the truck. "Let's just get inside, fast."

"Move that miniature motorcycle, Miles!" she yelled, climbing in behind the wheel.

I winced, sure that the Baxters and Man-Bear were going to come tearing into the driveway at any moment.

Miles grabbed Shelley and the wagon, which was no longer attached to the minicycle, and rolled them into the grass, glancing left and right like a nervous rabbit.

Mom parked, got out and headed for the front door. Lilith was right behind her.

"This is good," I said, trotting along beside them. "Let's all get inside."

"Wait!" Miles said, as we started onto the porch. "Wait! You could drive me back to the Baxters' house. We could get the camera. Collect the evidence."

"What's he talking about, Charlie?"

"They chased us," Miles blurted, before I could answer. "They attacked us. If we drove back in the truck, I could get the camera and show you the evidence, Mrs. Harker … I mean, Ms. Autumn."

"Who attacked you?" Mom asked, actually looking a little concerned.

"The Baxters," I said, glancing around. "Can we talk about this inside, please?"

"Why would the Baxters attack you?" She'd unlocked the front door, and her hand was on the handle, but she wasn't opening it. "What were you doing?"

"We were simply investigating their property," Miles said. "A routine investigation."

"With a video camera?" Lilith asked.

"We were gathering evidence," Miles said matter-of-factly.

"So, let me get this straight," Mom said. "The two of

you were snooping around the Baxters' property with a video camera, and you want me to call the sheriff because they chased you away?"

"They attacked us," I said.

"How exactly did they attack you?"

"Can I explain it inside?" I asked.

"No, you can't," she said, taking her hand off the handle and turning to face me.

"Well, you see, they had a friend with them, a big guy, and he grabbed on to my shirt while I was in the wagon you just ran over. He lifted me out of it with one hand."

"For the record, he was running beside us at approximately thirty-five miles per hour," Miles added.

"So," Mom said, her eyes narrowing, "you trespassed on our neighbor's private property, got chased away and then you escaped in the wagon?"

"It was attached to Miles's minicycle," I said. "The guy would've killed me, too, if I hadn't thrown Miles's video camera at his face."

"There's no way that toy motorcycle can go thirty-five miles per hour," Lilith interjected.

"It can go faster than that," Miles said, puffing out his chest a little.

"Charlie," Mom snapped, "you obviously annoyed those people by invading their privacy, and then you threw a video camera at their friend's face. It's a good thing I *didn't* call Sheriff Dutton."

"But they're not normal," Miles said.

"I'll admit it, Miles, it sounds like they overreacted," Mom said, "but I don't know how long you've been bothering them. Quite frankly, if you keep showing up around here at night, I might think about chasing you down the street, too. Especially if you start snooping around with a video camera."

"But —" I started.

"No! No buts," Mom barked. "Miles, go home," she said, pointing into the night. "Charlie, come inside. We'll work this thing out with the Baxters tomorrow."

"You can't send him out there now," I said. "At least give him a drive home."

"No," Miles said. "I can get home on my own. It will give me the opportunity to collect the camera on the way. Then I'll be able to show you the evidence, Ms. Autumn."

Before I could stop him, Miles bolted off the porch and disappeared into the dark. A moment later, I heard his Frankencycle sputtering to life again.

"Don't do anything crazy, Miles!" I shouted.

"I think you're too late," Lilith said and followed Mom inside.

I listened to Miles's minicycle chug and cough its way out of the driveway, and then went in, too, locking the door behind us.

"Leave the door unlocked," Mom said. "Johnny doesn't have a key."

"I'll wait up for him," I said.

"Fine," she said, "but I'm going to bed, Charlie. It's been a long day, and I'm dead tired."

I watched them trudge up the stairs, and then I scuttered into the sitting room and waited for Johnny to get back.

Saturday, 10:53 p.m.

Not long after Mom and Lilith had gone to bed, I dragged a chair over to one of the tall windows that looked out over the front yard and Elm Street. I sat down, waiting for Johnny to arrive, and I guess at some point I must have dozed off. It was Johnny's voice that finally woke me up.

From somewhere, way back in my mind, like a cloud crossing in front of the sun, I heard him saying, "Hey, dude, can I help you with something?" And then, in the same dark recesses of my mind, I was getting up, unlocking the front door and telling him to get inside. I could see the Baxters and Man-Bear marching across the lawn, straight at Johnny, their faces blank, their pointy fangs glinting in the moonlight. But I was already there, dragging him inside and locking the door behind us. Only, I realized I wasn't awake and dragging him inside, I was still asleep, sitting in the chair. I knew that — I knew I was still asleep. That's when I woke up.

I jumped out of the chair and looked out the window. A full moon was perched low in the sky, floating up there like a giant, glowing balloon lighting up the porch and the front yard. There was no one out there, but Johnny's motorcycle was parked on the edge of the driveway, beside the truck. That proved he'd been outside. But when? Where was he now?

"Charlie!" a voice hissed.

I jumped and realized I had to pee really badly.

"Charlie!" the voice said again, and Lilith slipped into the sitting room. "Did you hear that?"

"Hear what?"

"It was Johnny," she said, sliding over to me and glancing out the window. "He was outside."

"Are you sure?"

"Yes, he was talking to someone."

"Who?" I asked, but I had a feeling I already knew the answer to that.

"Come on, let's go," she said, grabbing my wrist and pulling me toward the front door. Before we plunged outside, though, I pulled back.

"Lilith, I wasn't joking tonight. There's something weird going on with the neighbors. I had a dream ... I think ... I think they were just here."

She furrowed her eyebrows and pursed her lips. "Then we should hurry," she said, yanking me toward the door and throwing it open.

The first thing I noticed was the utter silence. There weren't any crickets chirruping anymore.

"It's this way," Lilith said, and she pulled me off the porch and across the lawn, toward Johnny's motorcycle.

"How do you know?" I said, glancing around.

She pointed down, and I noticed a series of light indentations in the long grass that were clearly going toward the driveway. It looked like there might have been four or five people out here. Seeing those tracks made my bladder ache. If the Baxters showed up now, I was going to need a new pair of pants.

"There," Lilith said, pointing at a spot in the trees on the other side of the driveway where a few of the branches were broken and bent. "They must've gone in there."

"We should tell Mom."

"No time," she said, letting go of my arm and sprinting for the trees.

"Lilith!" I barked, but she didn't stop.

I didn't want to go in after her. I thought there were probably about five thousand better ways we could handle this situation, but I couldn't let her go by herself. So, foolishly, and with a bladder that threatened to explode with each step, I followed her into the trees.

"Lilith!" I hissed, barreling along blindly, hoping I wouldn't run smack into a tree. "Lilith! Where are you?"

She didn't answer, but I figured she must be close.

"Lilith!" I yelled, a little louder.

No answer.

My swollen bladder jiggled in my gut.

"Lilith!" I cried.

No answer.

I ran through a spiderweb and was busy wiping the sticky threads off of my face when I tripped over a branch and fell sprawling, face first. Thankfully the ground was covered in about an inch of spongy leaves and didn't do any damage, but I couldn't ignore my need to pee any longer. I jumped up and relieved myself, keeping a lookout for anyone trying to sneak up behind me. There were no angels singing this time; I was all business.

"Lilith?" I called when I finished. "Lilith!"

Nothing. No answer. Utter silence.

It was darker in the trees, with only slivers of moonlight flickering through the leaves.

"Lilith?"

She didn't answer, but I did hear a shuffling sound off to my right. I spun around, trying to see what it was, but could only make out the black silhouettes of the trees. The shuffling came again, behind me.

I whirled around, squinting, trying to pick up any movement in the darkness.

"Lilith, is that you?"

Shuffling to my left ... or was it from my right? I couldn't tell. I listened, I waited, my hands out in front of me.

"Lilith?" I hissed.

More shuffling, closer this time.

A shadow moved. A large shadow, about ten feet directly in front of me. It was too big to be Lilith.

"Hello?" I croaked.

The shadow flitted away.

I couldn't stand still any longer. I ran.

I sprinted through about a dozen spiderwebs, not bothering to wipe them off. Low branches swatted and scratched my face, I ran into trees, bounced off of them, staggered, ran some more. I trampled over bushes and through clumps of knee-high ferns. I ran and ran, hoping (praying) that I was heading in the general direction of the inn. But the trees never ended — in fact, they seemed to be getting closer together, blotting out most of the moonlight and smacking me with their leaves and limbs. I kept glancing back over my shoulder, always expecting to see the Baxters or Man-Bear closing in. I would have kept on running like that, full tilt, until I collapsed or puked, except I glanced back one too many times. One second I was hurtling forward through the woods, the next I was falling backward.

"That was a big tree," I groaned, and the world went from very dark to pitch-black.

Saturday or possibly Sunday

I don't know how long I was lying on the ground, knocked out. There was no way to gauge time in the woods. The only thing I knew for sure was that I was covered in mosquitoes when I came to. They were on my face, my neck, my arms, buzzing in my ears — they were everywhere. I sat up, swatting them away, and the ground tilted. Orange stars popped out of the darkness in front of me. For about five seconds, I thought I was going to pass out again, and then the world came back into focus. I rubbed the side of my head and felt a cartoonish egg-sized bruise under my hair. That's when I remembered why I'd been sprinting through the woods in the first place and slowly got to my feet. I scanned the trees for shadows and listened. The crickets were back, and about ten thousand mosquitoes were buzzing around my head, but there were no more shuffling sounds, and there were no more shadows. I was alone.

"Lilith?" I called, knowing that it was ludicrous to keep yelling for her. Lilith was gone. Heck, maybe she'd managed to save Johnny, and they were already back at the inn, kicking back with some cold pizza and a bottle of mustard, wondering where in the world I'd run off to. And that was an excellent question, wasn't it? Where was I?

I took a long look around, hoping I'd spot some lights

glimmering through the trees, but all I saw were more trees, and I couldn't even see a lot of them because it seemed to be getting darker by the second.

I swatted a mosquito that had landed on my neck and tried to think of a way to get back to civilization. According to all the brochures, Choke was the finest private school in the country, but they didn't spend a lick of time on what to do if you got stuck in the woods in the middle of the night. I added *complain about lack of survival training at Choke* to my mental to-do list and tried to come up with some way to get out of here before the mosquitoes drained me of all my blood.

Of course, if I'd had my phone, I could have figured out where I was with the GPS, or, oh, I don't know, called somebody to let them know I was lost in the wilderness. I tried to remember any movies or TV shows I'd watched that involved finding your way out of the woods, but anything that came to mind usually ended with the main characters being captured by serial killers or monsters — usually zombies — and I thought that might actually be the type of predicament I was dealing with, so I tried to think of something else.

I considered yelling hysterically, but I was still a tad terrified of being discovered by the Baxters and Man-Bear, and there was no guarantee anybody else would hear me. I thought about climbing a tree and trying to spot some signs of civilization, but the branches were either too thin or too high up for me to get a start. I did manage to make it halfway up one of the trees, but then I was attacked by some kind of rodent. It was small but surprisingly feisty, and I ended up falling most of the way down to the ground just to avoid its sharp little teeth. That's when I had to admit I probably wasn't going to make it out of the woods until sunup and considered lying down and sleeping the rest of the night away. It was tempting, except for the hordes of bloodthirsty mosquitoes swarming around me. It was only because of them that I decided to keep moving.

I didn't go in any particular direction, and I didn't do it fast, but it was better than sitting still.

Sunday, ?:?? a.m.

I walked all night, bleary-eyed, trying not to run into trees or trip and fall down. At some point, just as the sun was coming up, I heard the sound of water babbling over rocks and by some miracle I actually found my way over to the banks of a river. I plunged my face into the ice-cold water just to wake up a little. Then I took stock of the last twenty-four hours:

Severe sunburn — check.
Chased by neighbors — check.
Knocked out by a tree — check.
Mauled by mosquitoes — check.
Wandered around all night in the woods — check.

Things were definitely coming together, and as much as I would have loved to just collapse and have a long nap, I was still awake enough to realize that I might have stumbled onto a way back to the inn.

If this was the Rolling River, and judging by the icy, black water, I thought it probably was, then I could follow it until I got to The Bend. From there, it would be an easy walk back to the inn. Well, easy in relation to the amount of walking I'd already done that night. The possibility that I might be able to make it back to the inn and sleep for about seventy-two hours was more than enough motivation to keep me going.

So, using what was left of my willpower, which isn't all that much at the best of times, I stepped back into the trees and headed downstream. After about an hour of bumbling through the trees along the rocky shoreline, I stepped out of the woods and onto the shoulder of Elm Street. The river continued along, flowing under the road through a tunnel that you'd never know was there unless you'd been lost in the woods. I was hungry and tired, my feet hurt, my head felt like it'd been cracked in two, my legs were cramping and I was covered in mosquito bites, but the one thing I *wasn't* anymore was lost in the woods. I'd survived — barely, but I *had* survived. Now it was time to go home, or what counted as home for the time being.

Sunday, 7:35 a.m.

Elm Street was empty on my walk back, and I made good time as I trudged along the gravel shoulder. The sun was coming up and sending a faint haze of orange above the trees, the birds were singing and the sky was blue. Everything was absolutely peachy keen. Just the same, when I reached the Baxter place, I ducked into the trees. I don't know what I was expecting — a platoon of "zompires" keeping watch for me on the front lawn or maybe just another high-speed chase down the road? Only this time it would be pretty far from high-speed, considering I could barely walk, let alone run.

But there were no monsters waiting for me, no ambushes or chases, no decapitated bodies on the front lawn or apocalyptic fires blazing in the driveway. The Baxters' lawn was empty, their Volvo was parked in the driveway, just like last night, and the curtains were all closed. In short, the Baxter place looked normal. Normal enough for me to start wondering if I'd just imagined those fangs last night. Normal enough for me to think Mom might have been right about the Baxters and Man-Bear just being seriously perturbed about Miles sneaking around taking candid videos of them in their backyard. It was normal enough for me to consider whether Miles might just be a world-class loony tune who'd latched on to the new kid and actually managed to convince him something fishy was going down in Rolling Hills. Of course, that got me thinking about Johnny. Did he really get dragged into the night, or did he just go for a midnight stroll? There was only one way to find out, so I aimed my feet toward the inn and kept shuffling along.

It was already turning into another steamy day when I finally staggered into the driveway, scratching the five hundred or so bug bites that were covering my face, head, neck and arms. My Choke-mandated khakis had managed to save my legs, but I was pretty sure I even had a few bites inside my ears. As I turned onto the front walk, passing by Hal's pungent rosebushes, Lilith and Johnny strolled out the front door.

"You're okay?" I stammered.

They were standing in the shade of the porch, holding mugs and wearing sunglasses and ball caps. Johnny had on a Dodgers cap pulled low, while Lilith had opted for a plain black cap that was made out of the same high-tech fiber as the running gear she had on again. While Lilith looked ready to hit the road for a quick twenty-mile run, Johnny was bundled up in gray jogging pants and a black hoodie that made me feel ten degrees hotter just looking at him.

"You're okay?" I repeated.

"Of course," Lilith said in a flat voice. "Where have you been?"

"Oh, just getting the lay of the land," I said, stepping onto the porch.

"You're bleeding," she said and tapped her right temple.

I wiped my hand across my temple, sliding over an abnormally large bug bite, and pulled it away. It was smeared with blood.

"There were a few mosquitoes out last night," I said. "Do you think I could have a sip of your coffee, Lilith? I'm a tad groggy."

"Go inside and clean up first. Who knows what you came into contact with last night."

"You're a real humanitarian, sis," I said, scratching the back of my neck. "What happened to you last night, Johnny?"

"I came home and went to bed," he said.

"But how'd you get in? The door was locked."

"Through the back," he said.

"Did Hal let you in?"

"The door was open."

"Why didn't you wake me up? I was sitting right there," I said, pointing in the general direction of the sitting room.

"I went to bed," he said and sipped from his coffee.

That's when I noticed his hand was wrapped in white gauze.

"What happened to your hand?" I asked.

"I cut it."

"How?"

"I don't remember," he said, looking down at his hand as though it was the first time he'd ever noticed it at the end of his arm.

"But we heard you talking to someone outside — right, Lilith?"

"It was a mistake," she said and sipped from her own mug.

"Wow, you two sure are chatty. I had more lively conversations with the trees last night."

I was expecting Lilith to say something that was supposed to be wise, something that she'd absorbed from one of Dad's books, or for Johnny to say something like, "Chillax, bro, and enjoy the quietude of the morning," but they both just stood there and sipped coffee. I also noticed that their faces, under their sunglasses, looked wooden. Their mouths were practically straight lines. That was a standard look for Lilith, but the only time Johnny wasn't sporting a charming grin was when he was asleep.

"So, you just came back and went to bed, huh?" I said, backing toward the front door.

Johnny nodded and stared at me.

"You, too, Lilith? You didn't think about telling anyone that I might've gotten lost in the woods?"

"I knew you'd be fine," she said.

"How could you possibly know that?"

"We're twins, Charlie. I can practically read your mind."

They were creeping me out. Having them just stare at me like that — especially Johnny, who was usually all sunshine and lollipops — was seriously throwing me off.

"And you didn't see anything strange last night?" I asked.

"No," they said in unison.

"I think I'll go check on Mom," I said.

They didn't move. They just stood there holding their mugs, watching me.

"Why don't you just wait here and relax. I'll be right back," I said, opening the front door and slipping inside.

Was I thinking like a crazy person? Just because Johnny wasn't saying "bro this" and "bro that" didn't mean he had some kind of brain infection and was secretly sporting fangs, did it? No, it didn't, and it didn't mean anything had happened to Mom either. All the same, I bounded up the stairs toward her room. I'd only made it halfway up when she appeared on the landing at the top.

"Good grief, Charlie," she said, starting down the stairs. "What happened to you?"

"Do you feel all right?" I asked.

"Sure," she said.

"Can you give me a big, good-morning-sunshine smile?"

"Good morning, sunshine!" she said and flashed me a broad smile as she hustled down the stairs. "Good enough?" she asked, and it disappeared.

"Oh, that's great, Ma! That's just great!" I said, relief sweeping over me. Whatever was going on with Lilith and Johnny, if anything *was* going on with them, it didn't seem to be happening to her.

"No need to gush, Charlie. Now where are Johnny and Lilith? I want to go get breakfast."

"Out on the —" I started, but she stopped in front of me and grabbed my arms.

"You're covered in bites! What happened?"

"I spent the evening helping the native insect population with their annual blood drive," I said. "But that's not important. I don't suppose you've noticed anything different about Lilith and Johnny?"

"I just woke up, and don't change the subject. What do you mean you spent the evening helping the native insect population?"

"I might've spent the night wandering around in the woods, but that's really not important. What's important is where Johnny and Lilith spent the night."

"Do you mean you spent the entire night out in the woods?"

"Yeah, sure," I said, trying to get her to forget about me for a second, "but, Mom, where did Lilith and Johnny spend the night? Were they here?"

"We need to go to the pharmacy and get some cream for those," she said, taking a closer look at my arms.

"That sounds like an amazing idea, believe me, but

why don't we check on Lilith and Johnny first?"

"There's dried blood all over your neck," she said. "Have you looked in a mirror recently?"

"Mom, you have to check on Lilith and Johnny. Do you understand?"

"Okay," she said. "Where are they?"

"On the porch. But before we go out," I said, walking across the foyer, "they don't seem quite right to me. Let's be careful, okay?"

"Charlie, I'm not in the mood for jokes," she said, reaching for the door.

"Neither am I," I muttered, and briefly considered the possibility that Miles and Vortex were pulling off an elaborate practical joke on Charles R. Harker.

I was hoping Mom could drag more information out of Johnny about what he'd been up to last night, but the porch was empty except for two mugs, half-filled with coffee, sitting on the railing.

"Are they going to pop out and scare me, Charlie?"

"Possibly," I said, glancing around. "They were just here."

"Johnny! Lilith! I am not in the mood for a practical joke!" she shouted, stepping off the porch.

"Lilith! Johnny!" I yelled, sticking close to Mom. "Show yourselves! It's me, your brother, Charlie, and Mom's here, too! Don't attack us, okay!"

Mom stopped and looked at me. "Are you all right? Did you hit your head last night?"

"Possibly," I said, looking around for any sign of Johnny or Lilith. "Maybe we should just head into town. Heck, I bet they've already left for breakfast," I added, half-pushing her toward the truck. "We should probably go."

"But Johnny's motorcycle is still here," she said, pointing at his motorcycle, which was still parked beside the truck.

"They probably walked," I said, now dragging her toward the driveway. "If we hurry, we might be able to pick them up along the way."

I was 99.9 percent sure they hadn't decided to walk into town, but I was also pretty sure I didn't want to find them. Call it intuition or call it insanity, but my gut was telling me to get out of the front yard and into the truck, fast.

"I don't think they'd leave without us," Mom said, "and I don't need to be pulled along," she added, yanking her arm out of my hands.

"It's just that these bites are getting ridiculously itchy," I said, and scratched a few of them frantically. It felt like heaven.

"You're sure they're not inside?"

"Let's just get them some takeout," I said, scanning the trees beyond the driveway for any sign of movement. "That way we can get cracking on the renovations right away."

Mom glanced at me sideways and then shouted, "Come out, come out, wherever you are!"

"That's not a good thing to say right now, Ma. Please, let's go," I said, scratching my neck. "I need to get something for these bites."

"Fine," she said at last, and we headed for the truck.

Sunday, 8:00 a.m.

I made sure to check the backseat before we got in. I didn't want anyone springing up at us once the truck was on the road. It was empty, so I relaxed for a few minutes and was able to focus on scratching my bites while we drove to Church Street.

"Can you explain to me how you ended up spending the night in the woods, Charlie?" Mom asked, as we turned off of Elm Street and started down Oak Avenue.

"That's an excellent question," I said, scratching some more. Oak Avenue was deserted.

"Well, are you going to answer it?"

"Uh-huh," I mumbled, noticing, off to my right, that the front gate of a white picket fence had been torn off its hinges. It now lay in the middle of the perfectly manicured lawn. The old white house beyond it also had one of its front windows smashed out. One big, jagged piece still shot up from the middle, but thick brown drapes were closed behind it. In fact, all of the windows were covered up in that house.

"Charlie?" Mom asked.

A black SUV was parked right in the middle of the next lawn. All four doors were hanging open.

"That's strange," Mom said, noticing the SUV. "I hope everyone's all right."

"Yeah," I said, and noted that all the curtains and drapes were closed in that house, too.

The next house looked fine, and so did the next, although there wasn't a single one with a window open or uncovered.

Five or six houses down, though, there was a house that looked like it belonged on the set of a disaster movie. The front door was attached to the frame only by the bottom hinge and it was hanging open, most of the windows were smashed or had spiderweb cracks running through them, and two of the windows were completely gone. A blue minivan had run into the corner of the house, smashing the wooden siding and crumpling the hood back in a wedge.

"What in the name of Dolce and Gabbana happened there?" Mom said, staring out her side window as we passed.

"You know, I'm suddenly feeling like a bit of a drive this morning. Why don't we grab something to eat along the highway, maybe in the next town over. You know, try something new."

"Maybe I should call Sheriff Dutton to make sure everyone's all right," she murmured, ignoring me.

"That's an excellent idea," I said, as she pulled out her phone. Unfortunately, at that exact moment, a large yellow dog shot out from behind a bush and sprinted into the street.

Mom slammed on the brakes and dropped her phone. The truck squealed, and we heard a soft thump.

"Oh no!" Mom cried and jumped out.

I almost got out, too, but I stopped myself and took a look around first. This was exactly the type of situation I'd expect to see in some half-baked horror movie. The unsuspecting victims foolishly jump out of their car to check on a poor, innocent dog, only to be attacked by a secret mob of microchip-controlled, killer vampires. So, I gave myself a few good, hard slaps to the face, just to make sure I stayed sharp, surveyed the street and then slipped out.

The street was still — quiet, still and empty.

"Are you coming, Charlie? I could use a little help!" Mom cried.

"Be right there," I said, easing my way around to the front. She was squatting beside a golden retriever, who was lying on its side, panting and struggling to get up. It was obvious that at least one of its legs was broken, probably two.

"Easy, boy, easy. Just lie down," she said.

I surveyed the street, expecting someone to come outside, to claim the dog, to help us, but nobody came out, no curtains or blinds were thrown open, nobody peeked out of their front door to see what was going on.

"There's an address on his collar," Mom said. The dog was old. I could see gray hairs behind his ears and along his nose, and even though he was hurt badly, he was still wagging his tail a little and trying to lick Mom's hand as she read his tag. "It says 17 Oak Avenue."

"That's just over there," I said, pointing at the house directly to our right. It was a two-story brick house with ivy crawling all over it. The car, a big old Cadillac, was parked in the driveway. None of the windows in the house were smashed, and the white picket fence was intact (although the gate was open).

"His name is Mr. Chips. You need to hurry, Charlie!" Mom said, trying to keep Mr. Chips from getting up.

I scurried across the sidewalk and down the long

front walk, glancing around, watching for any sign of movement from inside. But there was none, not the slightest flicker or flutter from the curtains.

I pushed the doorbell, it ding-donged, and I listened. It was silent on Oak Avenue, no birds singing, no cicadas chirruping.

I listened more closely. Nothing.

I was about to ring again when I heard faint footsteps creaking down a set of stairs behind the door.

"Charlie? Is anyone home?" Mom yelled.

"Yeah," I said, taking four or five small steps backward.

Now shuffling footfalls were coming toward the door. They stopped, and I heard the dead bolt open. My heart rate suddenly skyrocketed, and the hairs on the back of my neck all lined up and stood at attention. The doorknob clicked, and then the door opened an inch.

"Hello?" a crackly voice asked.

"Uh ... hello," I stammered. The muscles in my legs had seized up, rooting me to the spot. "I'm ... well, I'm ... I'm afraid we hit your dog ... Mr. Chips."

"Mr. Chips?"

"Yeah, his tag said that this is his house."

"Yes, Mr. Chips," the voice said.

I waited for Crackly Voice to say something else, but only got about ten seconds of silence.

"Is Mr. Chips your dog?"

"Yes."

"He's hurt. Can you come get him? He's out in the road. I think his leg is broken."

The door opened another inch, and I could see the

silhouette of a short, hunched woman inside. I moved so she could get a look at Mom and Mr. Chips out in the street.

"Do you need help?" I asked.

"Bring him here," Crackly Voice said and abruptly shut the door.

"What's going on, Charlie?" Mom yelled. She was holding Mr. Chips by his collar, struggling to keep him on the ground.

"She wants us to bring him here," I called.

"What?" Mom said, confused.

"She's kind of old, I think," I said, jogging back into the street.

"Ask her if she wants us to take him to the vet."

I marched back to the door, ready to bolt at the drop of a hat, and called, "Do you want us to bring Mr. Chips to a vet?"

"No," Crackly Voice said, from behind the door, "bring him to me."

I turned and headed back to Mom.

"She says she wants us to bring him to her," I said. I scanned the street again. I had an uneasy feeling we were being watched.

"This is crazy," Mom said, motioning me over. "But we'll have to do what she wants. Help me move him."

We got our hands under Mr. Chips, me at the tail end, Mom by his head, and lifted him as gently as possible. He growled and moaned a little at first, but Mom shushed him soothingly and he quieted down.

Mr. Chips whimpered as we eased our way to the front door.

"Hello!" I cried. "We've got him! Hello?"

"Leave him there," Crackly Voice said.

"We can't leave him out here," Mom said. "Please, open the door so we can put him down — he's hurt."

"Leave him," Crackly Voice repeated.

"Ma'am, I can't leave him like this," Mom called. "He's in a lot of pain. I'll bring him to the vet and take care of everything, okay?"

The door opened a sliver and Crackly Voice said, "Bring him in."

Mom hesitated. She looked down at Mr. Chips. He whined.

"This is a bad idea," I said, looking at the darkness behind the door.

"We're new in town, Charlie," Mom whispered. "We can't afford to offend anyone. Remember, we need the inn to succeed."

"Inside," Crackly Voice said. Mom nudged the door open with her foot and it swung in on creaking hinges.

There weren't any lights on inside, but the sunlight slipped a few feet into a small entryway. There was a Persian rug on the hardwood floor and a round mirror hanging on the wall, which was covered in faded flowery wallpaper. Dust motes floated in the shaft of sunlight.

"Inside," Crackly Voice called. She sounded like she was standing well back from the door.

"I'm so sorry about this," Mom said, leading the way inside. That's when Mr. Chips started to whine again, whine and struggle.

"Easy, boy," Mom cooed.

We were inside now, standing on the rug. There were closed doors to our left and right, a staircase in front of us and a hallway beside it. There was a door at the end of the hallway that was ajar, and it was from behind that door that Crackly Voice called out again.

"Leave him there," she said.

Mom started to lower Mr. Chips, but his whining got worse, and she hesitated.

"I'm so sorry about what happened. My truck is right outside. I could take him to a vet and pay for everything."

I was feeling claustrophobic in there, like things were closing in on us and if we didn't move fast we might not get back out. "Let's just take him," I blurted, hoping for a quick escape.

"Leave him there," a second voice said. It was a man's voice this time, and it was coming from the top of the staircase. I couldn't see him from where I was standing, but judging by the sound of the voice, he was just as old as Crackly Voice.

"I've called Dr. Creed," he added. "She lives down the street. She'll be right over."

"Dr. Creed?" Mom said.

"She's a veterinarian," Crackly Voice said.

"And she's coming right over," the man's voice said.

"She'll be right here," Crackly Voice added.

Mr. Chips was whining and squirming more than ever.

"Let's put him down, Charlie," Mom said.

"Yes, leave him there," the man said.

"Leave him there," Crackly Voice added.

We lowered Mr. Chips onto the rug, but he didn't stop whining or squirming around.

"Your dog's very agitated," Mom said. "I think he's in a lot of pain."

"This will help," yet another voice said, from behind us.

I whirled around and found myself face-to-face with a woman about my mom's age, who was standing in the doorway holding a hypodermic needle. She was wearing a wide-brimmed straw hat and large round sunglasses.

"This will help," she repeated, but as she came in, she staggered and almost fell down.

"Are you okay?" Mom asked, grabbing her and holding her up.

"Just a little under the weather," she said, straightening. She was slim, was wearing jeans and had on a long-sleeve white shirt with the collar flipped up.

Mr. Chips growled and bared his teeth, but Dr. Creed didn't hesitate or stumble this time.

"This will help," she said a third time, bending down and quickly jabbing the needle into Mr. Chips's hip.

He tried to bite her, but his broken legs held him back, and she stood up as though nothing had happened.

"That will sedate him, and then I'll take him to my office," she said. Mr. Chips's growls were fading away quickly.

"I'm Claire Autumn," Mom said, holding out her hand.

"I'm Mariam Creed," the woman said as she shook Mom's hand.

"This is my son, Charlie."

"Hello," Dr. Creed said, turning to me. Her handshake was cold and limp.

"I'm sorry about all of this," Mom said, bending down and patting Mr. Chips, who was now lying still and panting lightly. "Please send me the bill for any treatment. We've just moved into the inn on Elm Street. Do you know it?"

"I'm quite familiar with it," Creed said, stepping over Mr. Chips and starting up the stairs. "He'll be fine now."

"I'm relieved to hear it," Mom said, grabbing my arm and pulling me toward the door.

"What do you mean when you say you're quite familiar with the inn?" I asked.

"Come along, Charlie!" Mom said, dragging me outside.

"We'll be seeing you very soon," Dr. Creed added.

"What's that supposed to mean?" I asked, but Mom shut the door behind us and pulled me away.

"What's gotten into you, Charlie?" she grumbled.

"Don't you find it a little strange that she's *quite familiar* with the inn? And that she threatened to come and visit us *very soon?*"

"I don't think that counts as a threat, kiddo — and we can't get lippy with the locals. We need them to be on our side."

"The locals aren't exactly —" I started, then stopped.

The SUV I'd seen with its doors open in a front yard was now parked in the driveway, doors closed. The minivan that had crashed into the side of the house had been backed into the driveway, and the front door that had been hanging by a single hinge was now propped back in place. It was as if a pit crew had rushed out and tidied things up while we were talking to Crackly Voice and Doc Creed. Was the whole street crawling with zompires? Were they all watching us right now? I flinched to the left and right, like a jittery chicken, and would have made a break for the truck, but there was a man sitting on a moped between us and the truck. He was dressed all in black and wearing a black helmet. The helmet's tinted visor was down, covering his eyes.

"Is this your truck?" he called.

"Yes," Mom said, heading toward him. I tried to hold her back, just in case this was the trap I'd been waiting for, but she slipped out of my grasp. "I'm afraid we had a bit of an accident, and I didn't have a chance to pull over to the side."

"It looks like there's been lots of accidents around here," he said, keeping the visor down. "What's going on?"

"I was hoping you could tell *us*," Mom said.

"A party gone bad?" he said, shrugging. "Although, Oak Avenue isn't exactly known for having a whole lot of out-of-control parties."

"Do you live around here?" I asked, keeping my distance.

"No, I live up on Birch Court," he said and flipped up the visor.

He was an Asian guy, with a gray goatee and round, silver-framed glasses.

"I don't suppose there were any strange goings-on up on Birch last night?" I asked, pretty sure he wasn't one of them, whatever they were.

"Charlie, don't start," Mom said, but he answered anyway.

"Now that you mention it, there was a bit of a commotion at the neighbor's place. I figured it might've been a few kids goofing around again or maybe some coyotes getting into the garbage."

"There are coyotes around here?"

"You bet," he said, smiling. "Lots of them."

I remembered all those shuffling sounds that I'd heard in the woods last night and felt lucky that all I had to deal with was a thick cloud of mosquitoes.

"I'm Bob Takahashi. I'm the pastor at St. Michael's."

"Claire Autumn," Mom said, shaking his hand.

"That's the place at the end of Church Street, right?" I asked, shaking his hand, too. He had a firm grip.

"That's the one," he said.

"You don't have a head cold or anything, do you?" I asked.

"I feel great," he said. "Although, if I don't get a cup of coffee before the morning service, I'm going to get seriously cranky."

"After what we just went through, a coffee would hit the spot," Mom said.

"Try the Frog Brothers Café," he said, starting up the moped. "They make the best cup of coffee in town. And stop in for our service at ten, if you get a chance," he added, lowering the visor and zipping away.

"What's with all the questions, Charlie?" Mom asked, getting into the truck.

"It just seems like there's a lot of people saying they're under the weather in this town," I said, getting in, too.

"Have you considered the possibility that they might just have colds? People get colds, you know, and they tend to be contagious."

"And it seems like a lot of people are walking around with sunglasses on."

"A lot of people wear sunglasses in the summer. You are aware of the existence of UV rays, right?" she added, starting down Oak Avenue again. "They're the invisible rays that turned your skin such a lovely shade of red yesterday."

"Yes, I'm familiar with UV rays, but people around here are behaving like robots, too. I mean, Mr. and Mrs. Crackly Voice weren't exactly social."

"Oh, wow — two seniors, living on their own, didn't skip out to meet the people who ran over their dog first thing on a Sunday morning. That *is* weird, Charlie. We should call the Welcome Wagon Police."

"And people wonder why I'm so sarcastic," I said, as we turned off of Oak and onto Church Street. The street was empty except for Takahashi, who was a few blocks up, parking his moped in front of the Frog Brothers Café.

"I think a little sarcasm is in order," she said, pulling up in front of Romero's. "I mean, is there a point in all of this, Charlie?"

"Look, I know this sounds crazy — I've questioned it myself — but Mr. Baxter, his wife and their giant friend chased us down the street last night. And his friend caught me and hoisted me up — with one hand, I might add — and then he tried to bite me. I got a good look in his mouth, Ma, believe me, and he had sharp teeth. They were like needles. I know that sounds insane, but I also know what I saw."

"Did you go to the Voodoo Juice Bar last night?" she asked, getting out of the truck. "I think we need to find out what goes into those drinks."

"They were running thirty-five miles an hour," I added.

"*Miles Van Helsing* said they were running thirty-five miles an hour, and he's the town conspiracy crackpot, according to Sheriff Dutton," she said, heading down the street. "Plus, you said yourself that you haven't slept much recently, besides the day before yesterday in the truck, and you might have had heatstroke from that burn you've got. You're tired, Charlie. You're probably not thinking straight. The pharmacy is this way."

"I admit it was dark, and I was keyed up, but you can't tell me something weird didn't go down on Oak Avenue last night."

"Sheriff Dutton said that the kids around here were going a little crazy now that school is finished for the year. Maybe the situation is a little more serious than anyone's willing to admit. Sometimes folks in a small town can hide their secrets, especially from the new family in town."

"Or maybe there are monsters running around attacking people in the night?"

"You've got to quit with this, Charlie. I know you don't like living here, but we're not leaving. This is where we're going to live from now on, come hell or high water, good neighbors or bad neighbors. Do you understand?"

"Home sweet home," I mumbled, stopping in front of the pharmacy.

Mom pulled on the door, but it was locked. "I should have known it would be closed."

"The sign says it opens at one on Sundays," I said, scratching some of the bites on my neck.

"We'll have to come back this afternoon," she said. "We're here now, though, so let's grab something to eat at Romero's."

"What about the Frog Brothers Café?"

"The coffee at Romero's is good enough for me," she said, and we headed back down the street. "Will your arms survive the wait?"

"I guess they're going to have to," I said and tried to resist scratching them again. I couldn't.

Sunday, 8:45 a.m.

Mabel met us at the door, holding a pot full of coffee and smacking her gum.

"How are you folks doing today?" she asked.

"Fine, Mabel," Mom said, as we made our way to the front counter. Although, we certainly didn't need to take a seat at the front, we could have sat anywhere; the place was practically empty. There were only two other customers, an older couple sitting in one of the booths at the back. They smiled and nodded at us as we walked in, and I noticed they weren't wearing sunglasses.

"Is it usually this quiet on a Sunday morning?" Mom asked.

"No," Mabel said, pouring us each a cup of coffee. "It's

usually just as busy as a Saturday morning. Something's going around. I never catch a cold, myself. Been working here for forty years and haven't missed a day."

Mom gave me a look that said I shouldn't start asking questions, so I let it drop.

"That's got to be some kind of record," I said.

"I take care of myself," she said. "For instance, I like to give myself a few sprays of mosquito repellant before I go out at night. The skeeters around here will eat you alive."

"That's a solid tip, Mabel," I said, scratching my neck some more. "I'll try to remember that."

"You should put something on those bites or you're going to scratch the skin right off your bones."

"The pharmacy doesn't open until one o'clock," Mom said.

"I think we've got some calamine lotion in the back," she said. "That'll take the edge off so you can enjoy your breakfast."

"Mabel, if you could take the edge off these bites, I'll work here for free for a whole week, just so you can take that overdue vacation."

"Don't make promises you can't keep, sonny," she said. "I might hold you to it."

"Hold me to it, Mabel, please. Just bring me that lotion."

Mabel smiled and went into the kitchen. She was back thirty seconds later with a half-used bottle of calamine lotion.

"So, when are you ready to start work?" she asked.

"Anytime," I said, slathering the lotion onto my arms.

"You know what, kid? I'll forget about your promise if you'll do me a favor."

"Anything for you, Mabel."

"Get a new shirt, that one's a goner."

"The first chance I get, I'm going to buy a spiffy new shirt, just for you."

"Actually, I've got one you can put on right now," she said, reaching under the counter. "Rolling Hills celebrated its hundredth anniversary a few years back, and the mayor at the time thought that making about ten thousand of these was a good idea."

She smirked and tossed me a white T-shirt. I unfolded it. *I ♥ Rolling Hills* was scrawled across the front.

"Rolling Hills has certainly impacted my life," I said, "but I don't think I can wear this, Mabel."

"Hand over the lotion," she said, grinning.

"You drive a hard bargain," I said. "Perhaps you'd be so kind as to point me in the direction of the lavatory, so I can change in privacy."

Mabel's grin got a little wider, and she pointed the way.

Sunday, 8:55 a.m.

I put on the T-shirt and slathered more calamine lotion onto my arms, which did wonders for the burning itch, but it made my arms look like I'd tried to paint them white.

"Will it soak in?" I asked Mabel, coming back to the counter.

"Afraid not," she said, "but the T-shirt looks smart on you."

"You're too kind," I said, sitting down. She *was* being too kind — that, or she liked her clothes loose and billowy, because she'd given me an XXL, which was at least two sizes too big. I didn't have the heart to ask for another, though, especially since I was planning on changing out of it as soon as we got back to the inn.

The service was fast, the food was good, and while we ate, I mulled things over.

"Did you notice most of the mess on Oak Avenue was cleaned up while we were talking to Dr. Creed?" I asked as we finished up our breakfast.

"They backed up a couple of cars," Mom said, shrugging. "I'm sure there's a reasonable explanation." She laid some cash down on the counter. "Let's go."

Mabel was pouring coffee for the couple in the back as we headed for the door.

"Thanks for the lotion," I called.

"See you later," Mabel said. "And put on some sunscreen, sonny."

"You got it," I said as we stepped outside. The day was already starting to heat up.

"Time to get back to work," Mom said.

"I'm going to grab a drink at the Voodoo first," I said. I wanted to pick Dr. Vortex's brain about all this, especially about that note he'd slipped me last night. "I'll meet you back at the inn."

"Not today, kiddo. I need you to mow the lawn, and I think those smoothies are turning your brain to mush."

"But my burn, and all these bites — don't you think I should stay inside and get some rest?"

"There's no rest for the wicked, Charlie. Now come on."

We were just about to get into the truck when Elizabeth zoomed down Church Street in her Porsche and pulled over to the curb.

"Wow, Charlie," she said, pointing at my T-shirt, "I didn't know you liked living in Rolling Hills so much."

"Sure, Winehurst, spending the summer in Rolling Hills doing manual labor has been on the top of my to-do list for years."

She rolled her eyes and turned to Mom. "How are the renovations coming along, Ms. Autumn?"

"Slowly," Mom said, "which is why we have to get going."

"What, no time to flirt with the prettiest girl in town?" I said. "How in the devil am I supposed to compete with Johnny?"

"How about dinner tonight at The Opal?" Elizabeth said. "Everyone's invited."

"Your dad is feeling better?" I asked.

"Yeah, a little, but he's still not quite himself. What do you say, Ms. Autumn, dinner tonight at seven?"

"Sounds nice," Mom said. "I need a break from takeout."

"Great! See you then," Elizabeth said. She slipped back into her car and pulled away.

"Announcing that you're flirting with a girl might not be the best way to win her heart, Charlie," Mom said, getting into the truck.

"I think I've been beaten to her heart already," I said.

"You never know how things are going to turn out," she said and started up the truck.

"Let's just hit the road. I want to mow that lawn before it gets too hot."

Sunday, 10:00 a.m.

Jake's red pickup was parked beside the inn, and he was sitting on the porch's front steps. His four-man work crew was with him, but they weren't sitting on the steps, they were all standing back in the shade of the porch, and they were all wearing sunglasses. I had a flashback of those guys at the Voodoo last night, standing along the wall.

"Sorry we're late," Mom called, getting out of the truck.

"No problem, but I've got bad news, Claire," Jake said, taking his ball cap off and wiping the sweat off his forehead. "The plumber's not returning any of my calls, so we won't be able to fix the water problems today. If he can't come tomorrow, I'll get someone from out of town."

"We'll get started on the main floor, then," Mom said.

"That's what I was thinking," Jake replied.

"Charlie, there's a mower in the garage out back. It's filled up and ready to go. Get cracking on the lawn, but put on some sunscreen first. There's some SPF 40 on the kitchen table."

Jake's men stared out at me with blank, wooden faces.

"Mixing sunscreen and calamine lotion might be bad for my skin, Ma. I think I should stay inside and help you guys out," I said.

"You'll be fine," Mom said, heading for the front

door. All of Jake's men turned their heads in unison and watched her climb onto the porch.

"I'm much better at interior design than yard work," I said, hustling onto the porch, too. Jake's men all turned back to me. I don't know if it was my heightened state of paranoia, but when they did that I felt something inside my head. It was as if tiny snakes were slithering through my brain.

"Nice try," Mom said, blocking my way in. "Go mow the lawn."

Jake's crew started crowding around us as they moved toward the door. They were big, burly guys who could easily overpower the three of us if they wanted to.

"I'll just grab the sunscreen," I said, tensing up.

"Fine," Mom said, and we all started inside — Mom, Jake and then me, followed by the Brawny Bunch. The last one in closed the door, shutting out the sunlight. I braced myself for an ambush, but nothing happened. They just stood like a pack of beefy robots in the foyer.

"Well, go get the sunscreen," Mom said, motioning toward the kitchen. "I've got things to go over with Jake."

"Right," I said, trying to think of some clever stalling tactic so that I could search the house for Johnny and Lilith.

"Well, go!" she barked, pointing at the kitchen.

No clever stalling tactic came to mind. I wasn't used to that — I'd been coming up with clever stalling tactics all my life, but I was too highly strung for the conniving part of my brain to function.

Mom sighed impatiently and marched into the kitchen.

I stood there in the foyer with Jake and his crew, who were all looming around me, staring.

"Quit staring at the kid," Jake snapped. "Jeez, you guys are acting weird today."

"Bit of a headache, boss," one of them said, and the others nodded.

"Don't nod all together like that. It's unnatural," Jake said and turned away.

"Right, boss," the same one said, and Mom came back with the sunscreen.

"Take it with you," she said, handing it over and grabbing my arm. "Reapply every hour," she added, pulling me to the door.

"Keep your eyes open for Johnny and Lilith," I said.

"Just mow the lawn, Charlie," she said and lovingly shoved me out the door. In the background, Jake's men kept staring at me with vague, empty expressions.

The door shut, and I stood there trying to decide what to do next. If I wasn't losing my mind (there was no guarantee of that), and there really was some kind of strange infection being spread around Rolling Hills, I was going to need a plan. Clearly, the people who were infected behaved a lot differently during the day than they did at night. For one, they used their words during the day rather than just mutely lunging at you with their pointy fangs. They didn't move really fast either; in fact, they seemed kind of slow and dull. And they avoided the sun, which made me think they might be vampires. Of course, that idea forced me to consider the possibility that I was indeed losing my mind, because, let's face it, vampires aren't real. Those were the mixed-up, wacky thoughts I was having when the sound of Miles Van Helsing's minicycle cut through the morning, and I knew things were probably going to get a whole lot wackier. All the same, it was a relief to know I wouldn't be alone with my crazy thoughts, and Miles would almost certainly add a few of his own.

About three seconds later, he coasted into the driveway, black smoke puffing out behind him. I walked over, but he didn't get off of his minicycle. In fact, he angled it away from me.

"What's that on your arms?" he asked, squinting and looking me up and down. "Is that zinc oxide? Are you shielding yourself from the sun?"

"It's calamine lotion," I said.

"So, you're saying the sun doesn't bother you?"

"I'm not infected with anything, Miles," I said. Leave it to Miles Van Helsing to make me feel like I wasn't paranoid enough.

"Do you have a headache?"

"No, and look, Doctor — I can dance, too," I said, pretending to tap dance.

He turned off the minicycle. "The camera was gone," he said.

"Huh?"

"The video camera you foolishly hurled at Igor Balic," he said, taking off his helmet and goggles.

"Igor who?"

"The extremely large individual you struck with my camera last night? His name is Igor Balic. I didn't go home and go to sleep last night, you know. I did research."

"I wish I'd spent my night doing research," I said, grabbing his arm and pulling him down the driveway. "Come with me. We need to check on my mom."

"I uncovered some extremely interesting information, Charlie," he said, trying to stop.

"We're going to have to walk and talk," I said, yanking him along. "My mom's in there with a work crew that might be —"

"Listen, Charlie. Igor Balic is the head of security for the Opal Corporation — he's an ex-KGB agent."

"The Opal Corporation?" I said, rounding the back corner of the inn.

"Yes, it's a multinational company owned by Victor Opal. Mr. Baxter is also an employee of the Opal Corporation. He's the chief engineer in charge of exploration and excavation."

"I thought Opal was into restaurants and resorts," I whispered when we were outside the back door.

"No, that stuff's just a side interest — it's not his bread and butter," Miles said. "Opal made his fortune searching for and finding buried treasure."

I put my finger to my lips to get Miles to stop talking, then eased open the door and skittered across the back room, motioning for him to follow me.

"Buried treasure is kind of a simple way of saying it," he whispered, slinking along behind me. "But that's what it boils down to. Opal tracks down and salvages ancient artifacts. Baxter's his man on the ground, and he just got back from their most recent dig a few days —"

He would have kept talking, but I made the international sign to shut up by running an imaginary zipper across my lips. He nodded, and I ever so slowly opened the door that led into the dining room. The hinges creaked a little, but the dining room was empty, and I didn't hear footsteps rushing toward us, so I figured we were in the clear — for now. We scooted into the dining room.

"Do you understand what I'm saying, Charlie?" Miles whispered.

There were two windows along the side of the inn, but the thick drapes were closed, so the room was shrouded in darkness.

"I think so," I replied. I could hear murmuring coming from across the hall. "Opal's a treasure hunter."

"Yeah, and Baxter just got back from a dig." He grabbed my shoulder, forcing me to turn and face him. "On *Oak Island*." He held up his hands and looked at me as if he'd just proven that the sun actually rotates around the Earth.

"Obviously Oak Island is supposed to mean something to me, but you're going to have to fill me in later," I whispered. "Right now I need to check on my mom."

"I think Baxter found something danger —"

I spun around and clapped my hand over his mouth. "Shut up!" I hissed through gritted teeth.

He gave me the okay sign.

I turned and crept toward the sitting room at the front of the inn, sticking close to the wall. The voices had died away, but I could hear a shuffling sound coming from what was probably the drawing room.

I peered into the sitting room. It was as empty as the dining room. I listened. People were definitely moving around in the drawing room. The floor was creaking, feet were shuffling, something went bump and then there was a grunt. It kind of sounded like people were struggling, maybe wrestling. Another thump. I pictured my mom and Jake being pinned down by eight thick arms, roped with muscle. I could see Jake's work crew holding their mouths shut, and then ... and then what? Would those fangs appear? Could they do that during the day?

I looked at Miles. His eyes were bugging out. "Who's in there?"

"They're infected," I whispered. My heart was thumping in triple time. "My mom's in there with them."

"We've got to stop them," he whispered.

I nodded and took a deep breath, but my heart wouldn't slow down.

"Do you have any wooden stakes?" Miles asked. "Or garlic?"

"They're all in my other pants," I said.

"This is serious, Charlie!" Miles hissed.

"Don't you think I know that?" I whispered.

There was another thud from the drawing room, and we both flinched.

"We're just going to have to battle them without garlic," Miles said. "Are you ready?"

I nodded, and like two half-crazed bulls, we rushed out of the dining room, through the sitting room and the foyer, then burst into the drawing room. My hands were clenched into fists, and my heart felt like it was going to burst out of my chest. I was a tightly coiled spring, ready to pop.

"In the name of all that is holy — STOP!" Miles commanded.

Everyone stopped.

But my mom and Jake weren't even in the drawing room — it was just Jake's crew. They weren't holding anyone down either. They were moving furniture. Two of them were carrying a long couch, another was moving a green, leather-upholstered chair. One of them was placing the antique dolls into a cardboard box. They were all looking my way. Surprisingly, their sunglasses were off — although it was pretty dark in there, with the drapes drawn.

"What's going on?" Mom said, rushing in behind us.

"I thought ..." I sputtered.

"Charlie, this is ridiculous. Why aren't you mowing the lawn?"

"I thought ..." I started again.

"Go," she said. "And, Miles, leave the drapes alone!"

Miles, who had been edging his way toward the drapes, hesitated for a split second and then lunged at them.

"Miles!" Mom bellowed.

His hands were an inch away from tearing them open when the guy who'd been packing up the antique dolls jumped up and grabbed him by his shoulders, yanking him back, away from the window.

"We're painting this room," he said, huffing as though he'd just finished doing the 100-meter dash. "We need to keep it cool."

I could see Miles was thinking about making another break for the drapes, but Mom stepped in front of him, blocking the way.

"That's fine," Miles said, looking around at Jake's men. "I found what I was looking for."

"Mom, can I —" I started, but she cut me off.

"I'm tired, and I don't want to see you until lunch, Charlie. GO."

"But —"

"Scram," she growled and pointed toward the front door.

I looked around at Jake's men. Besides the one who had grabbed Miles, they hadn't budged, although I noticed they were sweating profusely and their arms were starting to shake from holding up the chair and the sofa while all this had been happening. I had to admit, they didn't look like they were about to attack my mom.

"What about Johnny and Lilith?"

"Lilith came down and told me they're not feeling well. I'm going to give them the morning off."

"And I'm feeling well?" I asked, holding up my arms.

"OUT!" she roared and pushed me into the foyer.

"I'm leaving, I'm leaving," I said and walked out the front door, this time under my own power.

"Don't come back until lunch," Mom said and then slammed the door behind me.

Miles was already outside, standing by the drawing room windows. "That was a tremendous fact-gathering operation."

"They didn't bite anyone — that was good," I said. The adrenaline was still coursing through my veins, making me feel shaky.

"It's better than good, Charlie. They're slow and weak. The guy who grabbed me looks like he spends a great deal of time at the gym, but he obviously expended a huge amount of energy just pulling me away from the drapes. I think I could have barreled right over him if your mom hadn't been around."

"Are you sure about that?" someone said from behind me, making me involuntarily jolt forward and spin around at the same time. My adrenaline, which had just started to peter out, kicked in again. Lilith had managed to sneak up on us without making a sound. Worse than that, though, her face was blank, and she was sporting a pair of wraparound sunglasses.

"Hello, Lilith," I said, trying to sound natural, although I could feel a large vein pulsating down the middle of my forehead. "It's good to see you."

"The wise warrior remains open to all possibilities," she said, stepping toward me.

I didn't want to hurt Lilith, and I was definitely hoping she didn't want to hurt me. What would happen to her if I knocked those glasses off? Would smoke billow out of her eyes? Would she disintegrate in front of me? I wouldn't wish that fate on Stanley Peck or Bryce Wagner, let alone my own flesh and blood.

Miles, however, had other ideas.

"Heeyaw!" he cried, as he rushed past me.

A surprise attack like that would have worked against

any normal human being, but Lilith isn't normal. All her martial arts training has made her reactions lightning quick. She grabbed Miles by the collar, rolled and kicked him about six feet into the air. He flew over the porch railing and landed in one of Hal's thorny rosebushes. He let out a high-pitched yelp as he hit the thorns, and Lilith flipped back onto her feet.

"Watch yourself, Charlie," she warned and then darted to the end of the porch, sprang over the railing and disappeared around the side of the inn.

I considered going after her, but I thought even a weakened Lilith would be able to outrun me.

"I almost had her," Miles said, dragging himself out of the rosebushes.

"Not really," I said.

"Which way did she go?" he asked, staggering back onto the porch. His face was covered in a crisscross of tiny scratches. "We should try to track her."

"If Lilith doesn't want to be tracked, we're not going to track her — even if she's only at half power," I said, feeling my heartbeat finally returning to something resembling normal. "Besides, I should probably get started on the lawn."

"You're ... what?" he stammered. "We've got less than ten hours before sundown, and you're ... The *lawn*, Charlie? What the ...?"

"Easy does it, Van Helsing. I think you might've blown a gasket in your thinking machine."

"The lawn? Charlie, are you insane?"

"I was joking, Miles. I crack jokes when I'm scared,

nervous and confused. Even if there wasn't some outlandish, zombie-vampire invasion-type emergency going down, I'd try to get out of mowing this lawn. Since there actually seems to be some type of outlandish, zombie-vampire invasion-type emergency going down, I think the lawn can wait. But what can we do? Call the FBI and tell them they need to send their best monster exterminators here ASAP?"

"Well, I can't call the FBI," Miles said. "They have me on a list."

"A list of what?"

"The Chicken Little List is what they call it," Miles blurted, blushing a bit. "As if I'm some kind of fanatical end-of-the-worlder. All I've been trying to do is keep them informed of the paranormal activity we have in the area."

"What if I called and told them it was an outbreak of something, like a virus?"

"They'd call Dutton and Dr. Griffin to check the facts before sending anyone here. We'll need to show them concrete evidence before they'll listen to us."

"We're not going to try filming them again, are we?" I asked. "I don't think your minicycle's going to survive another chase down Elm Street."

"No, we're going to find something better."

Sunday, 12:50 p.m.

Against all the laws of time and space, I actually managed to squeeze onto the back of Miles's minicycle. The shocks were crunched together, the tires were bulging at the sides, and there was black smoke puffing out behind us, but we made it to the Baxter place without the engine exploding. About a hundred yards before we got to their driveway, Miles killed the engine and we glided onto the shoulder.

"Back at the inn, I started to tell you that I think Baxter found something down in that money pit on Oak Island —" Miles started.

"Hold up," I said, cutting him off. "Is this going to make me feel better or worse about what we're about to do?"

"I thought you might want to know that —"

"No, Miles. I don't want to know the nitty-gritty details about what Baxter found. Let's just go collect your evidence, get the word out and then hightail it out of this town. If we survive, you can explain it all to me on the beach."

"Fine," he said and shrugged. "I think our best bet is to approach the premises through the woods."

"Let's make sure we don't get lost."

"In these woods? Very funny, Charlie," he said and marched into the trees.

Sunday, 1:10 p.m.

We stopped and crouched behind a low bush. From there we had a clear view of the back of the Baxters' house. There were four windows along the second floor and three along the bottom. All of the curtains were closed. There was a wooden door, painted green, at the far end of the house. At the rear of the property was a small barn, which looked about half the size of a regular barn. It was painted white with green trim, just like the house.

"We have approximately seven hours and twenty minutes until sunset," Miles said. "Once the sun goes down —"

"Enough. I was there last night, remember? Let's just do whatever we're here to do."

"All right, we'll infiltrate the barn first and scour the place for evidence. If we get separated, we'll rendezvous back at my motorcycle."

"If we get separated in that barn, Miles, we're in serious trouble."

"The wise warrior never assumes that he knows the correct path," he said, then we made our way around the edge of the property, sticking in the trees, until we reached the side of the barn. "I'll go around front and open the doors. Keep your eyes peeled for the Baxters and wait for my signal," he said.

Before I had a chance to ask what the signal was, Miles darted out of the trees, skittered along the side of the barn and disappeared around the corner. I slunk out, too, sticking close to the wall, and examined the back of the Baxters' place a little more closely. In the light of day, it seemed insane to think that those two utterly unremarkable old farts might be lurking around inside, licking their pointy fangs and plotting the destruction of Rolling Hills. But I'd just spent the last year at Choke dealing with Peck monitoring my every move, so I was pretty good at sniffing out trouble, and my sixth sense was telling me to get away while I still had the chance. I almost made a break for it, but then Miles called out, "It's open!"

Despite my better judgment, I ran inside, too. I couldn't let him risk his neck in there alone. I don't know what I was expecting to find inside the barn, maybe a bunch of prisoners chained together or vampires hanging from the rafters, but I'm pretty certain I wasn't expecting a nearly spotless barn filled with shiny lawn-care equipment, all neatly organized against the walls.

"Help me get these doors closed," Miles said.

"That was your secret signal?" I said, helping him pull the doors shut behind us. "'It's open'?"

"I like to keep things simple," he said.

Once the doors were closed, there was only a sliver of light slipping in. Luckily, Miles had his phone, which he whipped out and switched to the flashlight function. He crept forward, scanning the floor with the light, until he'd almost reached the back of the barn, then he stopped and dropped to his knees.

"Here it is," he said. "A trapdoor." He grabbed a metal ring in the middle of the door and heaved it up. It swung open silently on well-oiled hinges, and Miles eased it against the back wall.

"Does every building in this town have a trapdoor in the floor?" I asked.

"Root cellars were common when many of the houses in this town were built," he said.

A wooden ladder descended from the opening in the floor and disappeared in the darkness below.

"A trapdoor that leads into a dingy root cellar is exactly the kind of thing I'd expect to see in a ridiculously predictable horror movie. And you know what else would be predictable and absurdly stupid ...?" I asked.

"I'm going down," Miles said.

"Exactly what I was about to say," I said. "I mean, have you ever watched a horror movie? Do you want to get killed?"

Either Miles wasn't listening or he wanted to get killed, because he was already starting down the ladder, his phone stuffed in his back pocket, leaving me in the dark.

"If you want to survive in a horror movie, Miles, what you do is leave. You hear a creaking door, you leave. You hear mysterious footsteps, you leave. You find a ladder that leads into a pitch-dark cellar, you leave. What you *don't* do is go down the ladder. The people who do that are the ones who don't make it through the movie alive."

"Charlie," he said, looking up at me, "we're not in a movie. Stay up there. Keep an eye open for Baxter."

"I think I'll keep *both* eyes open for Baxter."

"I'll be quick," he said and continued down the ladder.

When he reached the bottom, he whipped out his phone, flicked the flashlight on again and vanished into the darkness.

I could see the flashlight scanning back and forth down there, but that was all. I glanced back at the doors at the front of the barn. My danger-is-near instinct was in overdrive. If Baxter and his cronies rushed in right now, I'd be a sitting duck, and it suddenly occurred to me that the people who die first in horror movies *aren't* actually the ones who go down the ladder and do the investigating — the people who die are the ones who get left behind as the lookout. Don't the heroes always come back to find the lookout gone or dead — usually horribly mangled?

I glanced into the cellar and saw a few quick flashes of light snap through the darkness. Miles was taking pictures. I glanced back up at the doors and was about to go over and have a look outside when Miles called out in a half whisper, "Charlie, get down here! You've got to see this!"

"What is it?" I asked, but I didn't really need to know. I didn't want to stay up here waiting for Baxter anymore.

I scooted down the ladder and had just stepped onto the dirt floor at the bottom when I heard the barn doors creak open and sunlight flooded over the opening above me.

Miles grabbed my arm and yanked me farther into the cellar. Footsteps thumped above us.

"Here," he whispered, shoving his phone into my hand. "Get this to Mr. King at the *Daily News*. Their office is right above the Frog Brothers Café, on the second floor. Show him the pictures and explain what's going on around here."

Above us, the footsteps were moving toward the trapdoor.

"I'll lead them away," he said. "When the coast is clear, make a break for Shelley." He shoved the key to his minicycle into my other hand.

"We go together," I whispered.

"They'll think I'm alone. I'll meet you at the *Daily News*."

I was going to say I thought this was a ludicrous plan, but a shadow fell across the opening. Instantly, Miles bounded up the ladder and practically leaped into the barn.

He let out a bloodcurdling war cry, which was followed by a lot of shuffling above me. I could feel dust floating down onto my head. There was a crack, then the clatter of tools falling down, then footsteps pounding — and then it got quiet.

I waited.

I was alone, in the dark, but I did not need to pee.

Sunday, 1:30 p.m.

I inched over to the ladder and looked up. The barn doors were obviously still open because sunlight was pouring in, but I didn't see any suspicious shadows.

I listened.

Nothing.

I knew I couldn't wait down here for too long or someone might come back, so I started up the ladder, listening for the slightest noise. At the top, I poked my head up and quickly scanned the place. It was just me and the lawn-care tools, some of which were scattered across the floor. Had Miles actually managed to get away? Or were they keeping him gagged and bound somewhere until after dark?

I listened.

Nothing.

I crawled out and darted over to the doors, which were hanging wide open. The backyard was empty. There was no sign of the Baxters or Miles.

It was now or never, so I bolted across the lawn and into the woods. I didn't stop moving until I was back on the edge of Elm Street. Amazingly, I arrived at exactly the same spot where we'd parked the minicycle. I gave myself a pat on the back for my sharp wilderness survival skills, threw on Miles's helmet and goggles and started up the bike. It spluttered to life — what little bit of life it had left — and I pulled a tight U-turn. I didn't really want to drive by the inn and risk running into Mom, but there was absolutely no way I was driving by the Baxter house. Especially not on a miniature motorcycle that could stall at any moment.

Sunday, 1:55 p.m.

I didn't see anything unusual when I trundled past the inn, so I kept chugging along toward Oak Avenue. I figured the faster I got to Church Street and handed Miles's photos over to Mr. King, the faster I could get us out of this town. Oak looked about the same as it did the last time I'd passed through. The cars were all back in their driveways, but nobody had covered up the smashed-out windows, and most of the drapes were still shut tight. But Church Street was another story.

There were about twenty people, most of them of the senior variety, moseying along, smiling and chatting. But it wasn't the seniors giving me the heebie-jeebies, it was the dozen or so faces I caught staring out from behind some of the storefront windows. They looked like ghostly statues, standing back a few feet. They watched me drive by on the minicycle, their gazes following me from behind their sunglasses. I considered hightailing it down Church Street and straight out of town, just spluttering away in a cloud of black smoke, but when the Frog Brothers Café came into view, my conscience got the better of me.

I pulled over and parked in front of the café. I was going to go inside and ask how I could get up to the *Daily News* office when I spotted a sign screwed into the bricks at the edge of the building that had a black arrow pointing into the alley beside it. Below the arrow were the words *The Daily News — On the Beat in Rolling Hills since 1905.*

There were stairs about halfway down the alley. I climbed them to the door at the top, which had *The Daily News* printed across it in black letters. There was no lobby or secretary there to greet me. It was just one big room with boxes and stacks of paper scattered in piles everywhere. A couple of desks were near the windows that looked out onto Church Street. Behind one was a guy who looked only slightly older than me, typing on a battered black laptop.

"Can I help you?" he asked.

I marched across the room, pulled out Miles's phone and said, "I've got some pictures I'm supposed to show to Mr. King." It was only then that I realized I hadn't checked the photos first. In my mad rush to get away from the Baxter place I hadn't even glanced at them.

"He's out sick. Who took them?" he asked, holding out his hand. He looked tired, with scruffy brown hair and dark circles under his eyes.

"Miles Van Helsing," I said, handing the phone over.

He frowned but took it anyway. "What are you doing with Miles's phone? Did he finally get abducted by aliens?"

"Not exactly," I said.

I watched him scrolling through a few things on the phone's touchscreen, and his frown got deeper.

"It's a skull," he said, handing the phone back to me. "Where did he find it? No, wait — let me guess, in some secret underground catacomb on the outskirts of town?"

I looked down at the display.

The photo showed a skull sitting on top of a wooden crate. There were gray thorny branches growing out of the top of the skull and out through the mouth. They reminded me of tentacles — ones that belonged to a long-dead octopus.

"Is that a human skull?" I asked, feeling a little sick.

"Search me, dude," he said, turning back to his laptop. "How much did Miles pay you to bring that in to me?"

"He didn't pay me anything," I said. "We found it in the cellar under Mr. Baxter's barn."

He yawned and turned away from the laptop. "Well, there's your explanation right there. Mr. Baxter's job is to fly around the world digging up strange things so Victor Opal can make more money. You know he showed me a shrunken head last year? A real shrunken head! You see that stuff online, but you don't think you're actually going to hold a real one. That was seriously mind-bending, let me tell you. I think I washed my hands every hour for a week after holding that thing."

"What's growing out of it?"

"I don't know," he said, shrugging and turning back to his laptop. "Ask Baxter. But, look, word to the wise: don't listen to everything Miles has to say."

"That's probably sound advice, but haven't you noticed anything odd happening around town?"

"I haven't had time to notice anything. The editor in chief of this thing we call a newspaper has been out sick the last two days, so everything's on my shoulders, and I've got deadlines."

"People are wandering around like zombies," I said.

"Old-school zombies or the new style?" he asked, while typing something on his laptop.

"What do you mean?"

"Old-school zombies are pretty slow. The new ones are a lot faster."

"New style at night, old school during the day."

"Dude, half the population of this town is over seventy, of course they're going to shuffle around looking confused," he said, turning to face me and yawning again. "Listen, last October Miles rushed in here with 'irrefutable photo evidence of vampire activity in the area.' But you know what it turned out to be? Just a bunch of guys from the football team putting him on. Last summer he tells me there's definitely UFO activity going on near his house. I spent the entire night out in the woods with that screwball, and we came up with bupkis. Do you know what the mosquitoes are like in those woods?"

"I've got a pretty good idea," I said and scratched my arms.

"Yeah, looks like you do," he said. "The winter before that he wanted me to run a photo of a footprint he'd taken that he swore belonged to a sasquatch. All I'm saying is, you shouldn't listen to the kid."

"Yeah, maybe —" I started, but he suddenly jumped out of his chair.

"Wait a second! You're new in town, right?" he asked.

"Yeah," I said.

"What's your last name?"

"Harker."

"You're Johnny Harker's brother, right?" he said, rushing around the desk.

"That's right."

"My sister told me he was over at The Bend yesterday, but I didn't believe her. Wow! Dude, I'd love to interview him. Do you think you could set that up?"

"That's the thing. I don't think Johnny's feeling so hot."

"I could go meet him, he could come here or, if he's sick, we could meet at a doctor's office or in the hospital. Wait, is it serious? Let's just set this thing up, okay? My name's Jimmy Brooks. I'll see what I can do about the picture if you can get me an interview with your brother. What do you say?"

"So, you'll run it?" I asked.

"I'll need Mr. King's approval first."

"When can you get that?" I asked.

"I don't know. He's not answering his phone. I might

be able to run them in Tuesday's paper if we could set up the interview for tomorrow. What do you say?"

"I'm not sure?" I mumbled.

"If it were up to me, I'd print every single one of Miles's crazy photos if I could get that interview with Johnny, but Mr. King has to give the green light. Why don't you go downstairs, have a coffee at the Frog Brothers Café and I'll figure something out," he said, thrusting a five-dollar bill in my hand. "I'll run over to Mr. King's house if I have to."

"I can't stay long," I said.

"I'll meet you in half an hour, at the most," he said, ushering me back to the door. "Just don't leave, okay?"

"I'm not making any promises."

"That's fair, dude, that's fair," he said and opened the door.

I stepped outside and started down the stairs. Dark clouds had rolled across the horizon while I was inside, and they were heading our way.

"I'll be there before you can order a second cup!" he called.

While I walked down the alley, I took another look at the photo on Miles's phone. That human skull with a thorny plant growing out of it stared back at me. Was Jimmy Brooks right? Was it just another exotic addition to Victor Opal's collection of wacky artifacts? Yes, a few people were behaving strangely, and there'd been some vandalism to the houses on Oak Street, but that didn't mean Rolling Hills was ground zero for an outbreak of vampire-itis. Surely there were other perfectly logical explanations for the things going on around here. Unfortunately, I couldn't think of any, so I decided it was time to get advice from a person I often turned to when my life got a little out of hand: Richard O'Rourke. And since I had Miles's phone, I didn't need to resort to mailing him an *I ♥ Rolling Hills* postcard. I could just email him. Standing on the sidewalk just outside the Frog Brothers Café, I typed:

> Hola, O'Rourke, and greetings from Rolling Hills. I hope you're having a blast in your bunker. It's been a barrel of monkeys here! Did I say a barrel of monkeys? Actually, it's been more like swimming with sharks with some hard manual labor thrown in for kicks. Anyhoo, I'm writing because there are some strange things happening around town, and I'm not sure if I should be taking them seriously or if my brain has finally turned into Swiss cheese. I've attached a photo of a skull with a plant growing out of it that was found in my neighbor's root cellar. Take a gander, maybe show it to your old man, and drop me a line. This isn't a gag, like the time we sent that Photoshopped pic of Peck done up like a rodeo clown to Sterling. Believe it or not, this is legit. I think there's a distinct possibility that the people here are actually infected with something serious. Over and under, Chuck.

I pressed Send, even though the chances of O'Rourke taking this seriously were slim to none, and opened the door to the Frog Brothers Café. Thunder boomed behind me as I stepped inside.

The café was a small, narrow room with a few wooden

tables surrounded by chairs squeezed inside. The lights were low, and the place was empty except for three people sitting around a table in the back corner — I froze as soon as I saw them. It was the mannequin brothers from the Voodoo. I stared at them. They stared back, and I almost turned to leave, but a guy behind the counter called out, "What can I get you?" and flashed me such a friendly smile I felt silly about running out of the place.

"What can I get you?" the guy behind the counter asked again. He was short, with shoulder-length brown hair and a few days' worth of beard growing on his face. He was wearing a white T-shirt, and both arms were covered in tattoos. Standing beside him, drying off a coffee mug, was his identical twin. I think even their tattoos were the same. In fact, the only difference between them was that the one drying off the mug was wearing a pair of sunglasses.

The first guy caught me looking back and forth between them and said, "I'm Cory, that's Hamish. We're the Frog brothers. What can I get you?"

My danger-is-near alarm started buzzing as I strolled across to the counter. But I told myself there was always the possibility that Hamish and the mannequins had light-sensitivity issues. Maybe it was some genetic defect in people from Rolling Hills? Of course, they'd all have to be suffering from the mother of all light-sensitivity problems in these dim conditions, but it was a possibility.

"Ah, maybe ..." I said, stopping a few feet from the

counter and thinking again about leaving, but before I could take a step toward the door, two more people came in. They were both older men, probably in their sixties, wearing trench coats, fedoras — and sunglasses. The one on the right was leaning on a cane; the one on the left was carrying an umbrella. They looked like undercover spies from a really old and cheesy movie.

"I'll get you a cup of coffee," Cory snapped.

"I don't ..." I said, glancing from the mannequins in the corner to the undercover grandpas, who weren't moving away from the front door. Everyone was staring at me.

"It's on the house, and you *really* need to try it," he said, giving me a desperate kind of look that said he really wanted me to stick around.

"I guess," I said and felt a clammy sweat break out over my whole body.

"G-great," Cory stammered and cracked a false smile. "Coming right up." He turned around to pour me a cup. While I waited, Hamish continued to stare at me, still drying the same mug. It looked about as dry as it was ever going to get, and I wondered how long he'd been standing there like that.

My heart was hammering inside my ribs, and my lungs seemed to be constricting, making it hard to breath. Cory had his back turned to me and was busy doing something to my cup. Was he drugging me? Was he in on this ... this ... whatever *this* was?

I peeked over my shoulder at the grandpas. They'd silently taken a seat by the door. I figured this was my chance to escape. I could blow by them and be back on

Church Street before they could struggle back to their feet. Any ideas I'd been having about light sensitivity were gone. Any doubts I had about Miles were gone, too. I just wanted to get out of this place. I had to get out. And I was about to make my move, but when I turned to go, Dr. Creed, the veterinarian, appeared at the front door, followed by a huge cop. They were both wearing sunglasses.

"Hello, Charlie," Dr. Creed said, walking toward me.

"Hi," I blurted, and another clap of thunder sounded, making me jump.

"This is Officer Lennox," she added, speaking in an overly soothing voice. I imagined it was the voice she used just before she put someone's pet to sleep, permanently.

Lennox, who must have been six and a half feet tall, stared down at me from over her shoulder.

"Just getting a cup of coffee," I said and tried to smile, but I'm sure whatever crossed my face made me look more like a maniac than a regular happy-go-lucky patron of the Frog Brothers Café.

"You seem a little stressed," she said and nodded at my hand. "Be careful or you might break that."

I looked down and saw that I was gripping Miles's phone so tightly my knuckles had turned white.

"I forgot I was holding it," I stammered, and saw that the photo of the skull was still up on the screen.

"What's the photograph of, Charlie?" Lennox asked, turning his head a little sideways to get a better look.

Before I could answer, Cory Frog broke in. "Here's your coffee. Sorry it took so long."

I stuffed Miles's phone in my pocket and grabbed the large disposable cup, covered by a plastic lid, that was sitting on the counter in front of me.

"The cream and sugar are on the table over there," he told me and motioned toward the back of the room. "You'll *definitely* want cream and sugar. You won't regret it."

"Thanks," I said, thinking there was absolutely no way I was going to drink that coffee. In fact, I thought a better use for it would be to chuck it at Lennox's face and make a mad dash for the door.

"Add some cream and sugar," Cory said and glanced at my cup, then back at my face, then back at my cup. "You won't regret it."

"Right," I murmured. I didn't know if I could trust Cory Frog, but he was the only one in the place not wearing sunglasses, and he seemed to be trying to tell me something, so I postponed my coffee assault on Lennox and started over to the table at the back. My hand was trembling uncontrollably as I went, making the coffee inside slosh around.

I plopped the cup down on the table when I arrived, relieved I didn't have to see it shaking anymore, and popped off the plastic lid. That's when I discovered a note along the inside edge. It read: **Ask 4 washroom and then go out back door.**

I glanced over my shoulder. Hamish was still working on the same mug. Lennox and Dr. Creed were turned toward me, staring. The undercover grandpas were standing again. The mannequins, who were only a few feet away, were starting to rise. Cory was watching me, trying to look casual, but I could see panic in his eyes.

I read the note again. It was hard to concentrate on the words because the sound of my heart thundering in my chest was driving out any rational thoughts. I gripped the cream-and-sugar table, worried I might be on the verge of having a heart attack at the ripe old age of fifteen. I shook my head and focused all of my attention on the words Cory had scribbled along the edge. **Ask 4 washroom and then go out back door.** I wasn't crazy. Miles wasn't crazy. Cory Frog, an independent third party, knew something terrible was happening in Rolling Hills.

"Wahs sh wa srm?" I croaked. My mouth had gone so dry, the words came out sounding like mumbled gobbledygook.

"What's that?" Cory asked, his voice a little shaky. "You need to use the washroom?"

"Right ... yeah!" This time I shouted the words. Apparently, I'd lost all control of my vocal cords.

"Down back," he said, pointing at a hallway a few feet to my right. There was a sign with the word *WASHROOM* printed on it in large red letters stuck on the wall.

"Thanks!" I yelled. He cringed at my obvious panic. It made me cringe, too, because I suddenly felt outside myself, watching my body give in to hysterics. I gulped in air, trying to get ahold of myself.

"Just spread the word about the coffee, okay? Tell someone ... about what it's like here."

"Yeah," I grunted and took another gulp of air. I

somehow managed to put the top back on the coffee, despite my shuddering hands. I didn't want anyone to see the note.

"We need to talk to you, Charlie," Dr. Creed said, stepping forward.

"I have to poo," I cried, and broke into a half jog toward the washroom.

I don't know if you've ever had a dream where someone or something is chasing you and suddenly all your motor skills give out and you can't run anymore? Well, that's what it felt like during my sprint toward the back exit. It was as if all the muscles in my legs had turned to rubber, and they weren't listening to the commands my brain was sending them to go fast — extremely fast. I crashed into the wall twice as I ran along. The second time I almost lost my balance. I would have slammed headfirst into the door, but I managed to find my footing just in the nick of time and slammed into the bar in the middle of the back door with my shoulder instead of my head. The door flew open, and I went careening into the back alley, still by some miracle holding on to my coffee. I took a split second to look back and saw Cory tackling the mannequin who was leading the charge. Unfortunately, the others, including his twin brother, just trampled right over both of them.

"Run!" is all I heard as I skidded around the back corner of the building and started down the alley toward Church Street. I was hoping they'd give up the chase when I got out into the open, where the normal folks in town were wandering around doing normal things.

I was passing the stairs that led up to the *Daily News* office when Hamish Frog and Officer Lennox appeared behind me. Somewhere in the craziest part of my mind, I thought this would make a great photo op for Jimmy, and I actually let out a maniacal giggle as I sprinted along. My mind was whirling. Getting hunted down like this, in the middle of the afternoon in a small town, was so utterly unreal that I felt my grip on reality slipping away. It was like an enormous Hawaiian wave was crashing over me and pushing me under the water. I glanced over my shoulder again and saw Creed with Lennox and the mannequins. Even the undercover grandpas were in on the chase. They weren't quitting, but they *were* slipping farther behind.

I got to within ten feet of the mouth of the alley, and thought I might actually reach Church Street, when the Man-Bear appeared smack in front of me. He was bulging out of a gray suit, wearing a pair of aviator sunglasses and a ridiculous-looking straw hat. He had a bandage above his eye where I'd hit him with Miles's camera last night. I didn't have a camera today, but it suddenly occurred to me that I *did* have a hot cup of coffee. I'd been planning to use it on Lennox, but this was no time to play favorites, so I hurled it at Man-Bear. The lid popped off when it hit his chin and the steaming black coffee went splashing over his face. Man-Bear didn't scream, but he reeled backward, clutching his face, and staggered across the sidewalk.

I enjoyed about a half second of triumph, but Sheriff Dutton and Baxter stepped into the space that Man-Bear had vacated. I gave out a war cry of rage, mixed with absolute terror, and threw myself at them. At the last instant, Dutton pulled out a stun gun. It was too late for me to stop, and I practically fell onto the electric prods he was holding out toward me.

My body stiffened, and I fell to the ground. I only seized up for about five seconds, but that was enough time for Baxter and the Frog Café mob to pin me down. I was still reeling from the pain of the shock when Dutton pulled my wrists behind me and slapped on a pair of handcuffs.

Then I was hoisted up and carried over to Dutton's cruiser, which was parked beside Miles's minicycle. There were still a few non-sunglasses-wearing folks out on Church Street, craning their necks to see what was going on, but the black clouds were practically right over us now, and it looked like most of the sensible citizens of Rolling Hills had gone home to escape the rain.

When we reached the cruiser, Dutton opened the door and the people carrying me shoved me inside. Miles Van Helsing was slumped against the opposite window of the cruiser, unconscious.

"This will help," I heard a familiar voice say, and I turned just in time to see Dr. Creed jab my shoulder with a needle. I pulled away, but it was too late, she'd already injected whatever had been in the syringe into my arm.

"That will help," she said. Behind her I could see Man-Bear staring at me, his face blank but scalded a deep red.

"I'm not a dog," I said, but the words already sounded far away. The cruiser door slammed shut, and everything went murky. I looked over at Miles. A little bit of drool was hanging off his lower lip. Then I went to sleep, too.

Sunday, ?:?? p.m.

I was having a terrible dream. Johnny was standing in front of me, big vampire fangs jutting out of his mouth, yelling, "Charlie, wake up!" Then he slapped my face. Then he yelled, "Charlie, wake up!" I knew he was going to slap me again — I could see his hand coming, but my arms were so heavy, I couldn't do anything to stop him. Slap!

"Charlie, wake up!" he said again, but this time someone else's voice was coming out of his mouth.

"Don't hit me," I mumbled, but he slapped me again anyway.

"Charlie," the voice said, "wake up!"

It sounded like the voice was coming from behind me now, so in my dream I turned around, and that's when my eyes opened a crack. Miles Van Helsing's face was looking down at me.

"Miles?" I said, trying to remember what was going on. "Were you just hitting me?"

"It was more like a gentle tap," he said.

"Where am I?" I asked, sitting up.

"In jail," Miles said, although, now that I was awake and looking around, I didn't really need him to answer. We were in a small jail cell, the kind you see on TV all the time where the perps are held while they wait for their lawyers. There was a wall of bars along the front, and the rest of the place was painted a drab gray. I was sitting in the middle of the floor with Miles kneeling beside me. Behind him, a wooden bench ran along the wall.

"These are the holding cells in the basement of the Rolling Hills police station."

"How'd they catch you?" I asked.

"After we split up, I tried to make it back to my house. It's only half a mile from the Baxters', an easy run. I've got some security cameras set up outside, for day-to-day surveillance purposes, and I was hoping I could catch Baxter chasing me. It wouldn't be as significant as the material we caught on film last night, but I thought it might add to the evidence we've already compiled."

"But he ran you down?"

"No, I lost him pretty quickly, but Dutton and Mrs. Baxter were waiting for me at home. They were talking to my mother in the living room."

"What?"

"Mrs. Baxter had told her that I'd been harassing them. Dutton said he wanted to have a chat with me back at the station, just to make sure I didn't get into the same kind of trouble as last summer."

"What did you do last summer?"

"There was some paranormal activity in the area. I may have gotten a little carried away, but it's all water under the bridge."

"Your mom actually let them take you away?"

"Other than the fact that they never removed their sunglasses, they were acting normal — which is immensely worrying, Charlie. It means they'll be capable of moving around among us without arousing suspicion."

"But your mom just let them haul you away?"

"Like I said, last summer I may have gotten a little too fanatical," he said, running his hand through his hair. "I didn't want to upset her again, so I went along quietly, thinking I'd be able to slip away at some point. Unfortunately, I hadn't counted on them planning ahead. Dutton stopped at Dr. Creed's house on Maple and picked her up, along with Igor Balic. Balic and Dutton held me still while she administered some kind of tranquilizer."

"She did the same to me," I said.

"But at least you got the pictures to Mr. King at the paper," Miles said. "That gives us a shred of hope, anyway."

"Actually, Mr. King's been sick."

"You didn't talk to Jimmy Brooks, did you?"

I nodded.

"Crud! He's never forgiven me for the night we spent out in the woods!" he said, standing up. "What kind of idiot spends the night in the woods without mosquito repellant?"

"It's hard to be prepared for everything, Miles," I said. "But even if Jimmy put the pictures in the paper, what are people supposed to think about a skull with a thornbush growing out of it?" I said, standing up, too. "I mean, what is that thing anyway?"

"How should I know?" Miles exclaimed, throwing his arms up. "It might be a plant, an animal, a fungus, a brain-eating parasite ..."

"A brain-eating parasite?"

"Have you ever heard of neurocysticercosis? It's spread

when people eat pork that's been handled by someone with human feces on their hands."

"Stop, Miles. You're making me hungry."

"It's no joke, Charlie!" Miles said, running his hands through his hair again. "Basically, it's the larva of a tapeworm that gets into your brain and lives inside a cyst, feeding on your cerebral cortex. Millions of people are infected all over the world. Or how about *Naegleria fowleri*?"

"I don't think I need to hear about that one."

"Technically, it's an amoeba, not a parasite. It lives in lakes and rivers and gets into your body through your nose. Then, it gradually makes its way into your brain, where it starts eating the neurons in your frontal lobe, which controls reasoning and emotions. You usually die within a week."

"Don't you think people would know about a thornbush infection that turns people into fang-sprouting monsters? I mean, wouldn't there be a health warning?"

"Not necessarily. We're discovering new species of plants and animals and new viruses and parasites all the time. Not that long ago, a prehistoric cave in the Middle East was cracked open and a whole slew of —" he started, but stopped suddenly. "Did you hear that?" he asked, stepping over to the bars.

I followed him over and listened. "Hear what?" I said — and then I heard it. Raspy breaths.

"Hello?" Miles called. "Hello, is someone there?"

There was a hallway, lit by flickering fluorescent lights, in front of our cell that stretched to our left and right.

"Hello!" I shouted. "Is anyone there?"

"Easy, Charlie," Miles muttered, looking up at the ceiling. "We don't want to bring anyone down to check on us."

"Over here," a hoarse voice called.

I jammed my face as far as it would go through the bars and looked to our left. A tattooed arm was sticking out into the hallway and waving.

"Is that you, Cory?" I asked. "Cory Frog?"

"It's me," he said. "Who are you?"

"The guy you tried to help escape from the café."

"They caught you," he groaned. "That's a bummer."

"Afraid so," I said. "Hey, how'd you know what was happening, anyway? Everyone else in town seems oblivious."

"When I got to work this morning, my brother was acting kind of off, you know? He said he had a bad headache, so I let it slide, but by lunch I was fed up and told him I was going to get the doctor. That's when those three guys who were sitting in the back stalked in and started ordering drinks. Every time I tried to leave, they ordered something else. A couple of times I tried to sneak out the back, but Hamish kept getting in the way. After a few hours of that, I was feeling kind of trapped and ready to make a break for it myself, but I didn't want to leave Hamish behind. That's when you came in."

"I'm Charlie, and Miles Van Helsing is over here with me. Thanks for trying. Your plan almost worked."

"No problem," Cory croaked. "Do you guys have a plan for getting out of here?"

I scanned our cell. There were no loose-looking bars,

no air ducts or grates we could wiggle into and there were no keys hanging on the hallway wall.

"We're locked up tight. I don't suppose you've been secretly digging a tunnel through the wall while we've been talking?" I said to Cory.

Miles let out a growl. "This is no time for your infernal jokes!" he cried, grabbing my shoulders and shaking me. "There's no way out of here! They're up there somewhere and —" The sound of a door opening, somewhere off to our right, cut him off.

"That's not good," I mumbled.

"No, it's not," Miles said, letting me go.

Footsteps started down the stairs. By the sound of things, more than one person was coming our way. We backed away from the bars. My heart was pounding.

"If they come in here, attack them and don't let up," Miles whispered. "Our only chance is to overpower them while the sun's still up."

"Is the sun still up?" I asked. "Do you know what time it is?"

"Holy Albert Einstein — you're right. I don't know what time it is!" Miles said, his eyes getting wide. "They took my watch."

"And they took your phone away from me, too," I said.

The footsteps had reached the bottom, and they were getting closer.

"If it is after dark, and they've changed," Miles said, "I'll throw myself at them. You make a break for it."

"We're getting out of this together," I said, and then Sheriff Dutton appeared, moving like a regular person.

Lennox came next, and behind him was Mr. Baxter. Between them was a wooden crate they were carrying on a stretcher.

"Oh, crud," Miles groaned, and then Victor Opal strode in behind them all. He was wearing an expensive-looking black suit and had his mirrored sunglasses on.

"I thought," Opal started, sounding a little winded, "I would show you what we found, Mr. Van Helsing, since you were so interested."

Lennox and Baxter stopped in front of our cell and lowered the crate to the ground.

"That wasn't necessary," Miles said, his voice quavering.

"Oh, but it's so fascinating," Opal said as Baxter pried the top off the crate. "My associate here, Ted Baxter, unearthed it in a place called Oak Island in Nova Scotia. There's a long story about how it got there, but to make a long story short, you just have to understand that the pirates who buried it didn't understand what they were doing. They were robbing the world of something wonderful, and all because of their silly superstitions and old wives' tales about bloodsucking monsters."

Opal paused while Lennox reached into the crate and pulled out the skull. Lennox gently eased it onto the floor of the hallway, right in front of our cell. It didn't look exactly the same as before, it looked more alive — the branches looked thicker and appeared to be covered in tiny red dots. I had this terrible sinking feeling in my stomach, a nauseous swirling that made me turn away. But as I did, I noticed that Sheriff Dutton was wearing a ring of keys, clipped to his belt.

"Something wonderful?" Miles spat. "Do you think whoever's skull that was thought it was wonderful?"

"In his time, yes," Opal said, remaining expressionless, like he was making this speech in his sleep. "But unfortunately, the things that shine the brightest in life are often extinguished the fastest."

"Just as I thought," Miles exclaimed, taking a step forward. "The infection wastes you away. It's no symbiotic relationship — it's just a simple parasite that sucks the life out of you. And when it's done, it bursts out of the host, looking for a new home!"

"That's a simpleminded way of looking at it," Opal said. "But soon you will join us, and then you will understand."

"That's not going to happen!" Cory roared from next door.

"You *will* join us," Opal said, and Baxter put the top back on the empty crate. "Just like your brother. And yours," he added, turning to me.

"How long do you get to live before that thing starts to use your skull as its flowerpot?" I asked, easing my way toward the front of the cell again. Dutton was standing within arm's reach. If I could get close enough, I might be able to snatch those keys away.

"All your questions will be answered soon," Opal said. "There's not much time until sundown, then the blossoms will awaken. Of course, there are other methods we could use, but we thought Mr. Van Helsing would be interested in seeing how it all began."

Lennox and Baxter picked up the stretcher with the crate on it, leaving the skull sitting on the floor in front of them. I didn't want to even pretend to touch it, but I thought if I made a threatening move toward it, Dutton's police instincts might kick in and he'd try to protect it. In order to do that he'd have to come close to the bars, and then I might be able to grab his keys.

"I'll kill it!" I cried, rushing forward.

I shot my arm through the bars and reached for the skull. That gave me a close-up look at the branches. The blossoms looked like minuscule red spiders. There were thousands of them, stuck to the branches, and I flinched slightly but fought the instinct to pull away. Most of them were trembling back and forth, like they were trying to detach themselves.

"Get back," Dutton said flatly, squatting beside the skull and sliding it away.

I reached my other arm through the bars and grabbed the ring of keys. I pulled them off his belt, wheeling backward away from the bars. Unfortunately, the keys were attached to a cord, which came whirring out of a small box-like gadget that was attached to his belt. The cord unwound for about three or four feet and then stopped. Dutton, who'd been mid-squat, was caught off guard and fell into the bars

"Stop that," Opal said, and I thought his voice almost sounded angry. "You cannot prevent the inevitable."

"Hand them over," Lennox added, lowering the crate with Baxter.

"Come on and get them," Miles exclaimed, grabbing on to the cord, too.

Dutton tried to stand up, but we yanked the cord again and he stumbled back into the bars. It's ridiculous, considering the circumstances, but I actually thought to myself that I should add *find out what kind of key-reel-doohickey that is* to my mental to-do list. It was amazingly strong. O'Rourke and I had once used something like it to try to rappel down the side of Weaver Hall, and the cord had snapped almost immediately.

While those slightly insane thoughts were flashing through my mind, Lennox, who had a ring of keys of his own, marched toward the cell door. He pulled the keys away from his belt and an identical cord whirred out of an identical gadget.

"What's happening?" Cory yelled from his cell.

"Be calm, Mr. Frog," Victor Opal said. "This will only take a moment."

"Be ready when the door opens," Miles whispered to me.

My whole body tensed as Lennox slipped the key into the lock. He turned it, the bolt clicked and he pulled the door open an inch.

"Now!" Miles cried and charged at the cell door. He caught me a little off guard, but I still managed to ram into the bars right behind him.

Lennox was caught off guard, too, and under ordinary circumstances he would have been able to hold us back, but he was weaker than normal. So, when we plowed into the door, he stumbled across the hall and crashed into the opposite wall, and the door swung open, sweeping the skull to the side.

"That was a foolish thing to do," Opal said, and he closed in on us with Baxter, while Dutton and Lennox started to get up off the floor.

"Do your worst!" Miles yelled, his fists up.

Opal took another step forward, and I braced myself for a fight, but then he froze and stood very rigid. The fingers on his hands stretched out, his jaw clenched, the muscles in his neck popped.

"What the ..." I began, and then Opal and the others dropped onto the ground, shuddering. It was as if they'd all been electrocuted at the same moment.

"Quick!" Miles cried, grabbing my wrist and dragging me forward.

I stepped over Dutton, who was still shuddering beside the skull. As I did, I saw a single red dot float by my face. I blinked, thinking I was imagining things, but the red dot didn't disappear. Then I noticed another and another, only now I could see they weren't just dots, they were the tiny red spider blossoms that had been attached to the thornbush thing. I glanced down and saw thousands of them, all floating into the air. But they weren't just aimlessly floating, they were converging on us in cloudy swarms. I saw one land on Miles's forearm. He slapped at it, and a squirt of red goo, way more goo than I was expecting for something so small, shot across his arm.

"Cover your mouth and nose," he said, cupping one of his hands over the lower half of his face and wiping away the goo on his shirt.

"What's happening?" Cory Frog yelled from his cell.

We rushed over to him as hundreds of the spider blossoms floated off the thornbush.

"The keys!" he screamed. "Where are the keys?"

I dashed back to Dutton, crashing through one of the

red swarms. A bunch of them stuck on to my shirt. I grabbed the keys with one hand, keeping the other hand locked over my nose and mouth, and frantically swiped at them with the keys. Red goo splattered across the front of my shirt. Were they on my eyes? In my ears? I couldn't tell. It felt like tiny insects were crawling all over me.

I darted back toward the cell, the cord whirring out again.

"Quick!" Cory cried.

I got within a foot of the lock when the cord stopped. I yanked on it, but it wouldn't go any farther.

"Hurry!" Cory screamed. "Unlock it."

Miles sprinted over to Dutton and started dragging him along the floor toward Cory's cell. The sheriff was hardly trembling anymore. I didn't think that was a good sign.

"Let me out of here!" Cory said, shaking the cell door, his eyes wild with fear.

"Cover your mouth and nose," Miles said, rushing back, while I tried the first of four keys on the ring.

"Faster!" Cory howled. "They're getting up!"

The first key didn't work, and I tried the next one, glancing down the hall. He was right — Dutton, Baxter, Lennox and Opal were easing onto their knees, like boxers who'd been knocked down and were trying to beat the knockout count.

"You've got to get me out of here!"

"Cover your mouth!" Miles hollered, but it was too late. Just as Cory was about to scream about the keys again, he inhaled some of those spider things. I saw a small cluster of them go whirling into his mouth. A look of utter surprise crossed his face. He coughed, and red goo dribbled from the corner of his mouth.

"Let me —" he started, and then grabbed on to his throat, like he was choking. "Let —" he coughed, but his eyes rolled up in his head and he dropped to the ground, shuddering.

"This is worse than I thought!" Miles exclaimed. "The infection works almost instantly."

"It doesn't matter anymore!" I cried. "We've got to move!"

Dutton was half-standing when we started down the hall, spider blossoms hitting my face and sticking onto my *I ♥ Rolling Hills* shirt. I wiped at them desperately, smearing red goo across my shirt and hands again. I hip-checked Dutton as I passed by, sending him crashing onto the ground. Miles shoved Lennox into our old cell, and the big man stumbled and fell. Baxter and Opal clutched at us weakly, but we broke out of their grip. At least their superhuman speed and strength hadn't kicked in yet.

Two seconds later, we were standing at the end of the hallway, looking up a set of stairs. There was a door at the top, which was closed.

"Please be unlocked, please be unlocked ..." I prayed as we scrambled up, both of us wildly wiping our faces and hair.

Miles reached the top first. He grabbed the doorknob and twisted. The door swung open, and I've never felt such a strange mixture of doom and joy at the same time. I didn't know if I should be screaming or dancing a quick jig. Instead, I giggled uncontrollably. I looked back and Victor Opal was standing at the bottom of the stairs, staring up at me. His sunglasses were gone, and his eyes were wide. He pulled back his lips in a snarl and revealed a mouthful of sharp fangs. In the flickering fluorescent lights, I thought I could see tiny red dots on those fangs. I was pretty sure that one bite from Victor Opal, and a dozen of those creepy little things would be slipping under my skin and crawling through my veins.

"Harker!" Miles roared, grabbing me by the shirt collar and yanking me through the door. Baxter was behind Opal now, and they started taking quick, jerky steps up the stairs.

I slammed the door shut just as Miles grabbed on to the nearest desk and started pushing it toward me.

"Hurry!" I cried and leaned my back against the door, holding the knob. The knob violently twisted out of my grip, and I felt the door shoot open a few inches. Miles practically threw the desk the last few feet, and I leaped out of the way, narrowly avoiding being pinned. The door didn't slam shut, though. Instead, there was a squishing crunch, and I saw that four fingers had gotten in the way of it closing completely. They straightened out reflexively and then went limp, but nobody screamed in pain from the other side.

"Outside!" Miles yelled.

There was another door across the room, and beside it was a large window that looked out onto an empty street. Rain was pouring down, and the streetlights were on. We rushed to the door and out onto the sidewalk. The rain was coming down in sheets, soaking me almost immediately. Washing what remained of the spider blossoms off me, I hoped.

"Where are we?" I asked. We weren't on Church Street anymore, although the brick buildings looked similar.

"We're on Beech Street," Miles said, looking up and down the empty road.

I knew we had to move fast but had no idea which way to go.

"We need to hide," Miles said, starting to run down the street. "Then we'll figure things out."

Before we'd gone ten yards, Dr. Creed emerged a block away, with about a half dozen other people. I recognized Hamish Frog among them.

We turned to go in the other direction, but Opal and his gang rushed out of the police station, blocking our path.

We pressed together, back-to-back. A half dozen more people filed out of the Rolling Hills public library across the street. The brown-eyed girl from the Voodoo was one of them.

"Were they all just waiting for us?" I cried.

"Hive mind!" Miles exclaimed. "Telepathic communication!"

"I don't think we have long before we're going to be forced to join the hive."

"Or colony," Miles said, as the three groups closed in on us.

"I've never been a big fan of hives *or* colonies," I said breathlessly, the rain dripping off of me. "I'm not really a joiner, you know?"

Before we could decide on our next move, a red Porsche squealed onto Beech Street.

We froze, along with everybody else. For an instant, the only thing that was moving was Elizabeth's Porsche, and it was hurtling straight at us.

Dutton was the first one to react. He marched into the middle of the street, his hand up in front of him.

"Don't stop," I muttered. "Please don't stop."

The car was maybe twenty-five yards from Dutton and closing in fast when the group from the library and Lennox marched into the street to join him, all holding their hands out in front of them.

"Don't stop!" I screamed, just as someone grabbed my shoulder from behind and spun me around.

It was Dr. Creed. She was snapping at me with jagged fangs that were crawling with little red dots. She would have bitten me, too, if Miles hadn't grabbed me and thrown me to the ground. I thought Creed was going to pounce on us, but there was a long honk and a loud, screeching skid, followed by a series of thumps. Creed staggered backward, along with all the others in her group.

"Quick!" someone shouted.

I looked up and saw Elizabeth's car about ten feet away. The windshield was cracked, and there was a dent in the hood. Jimmy Brooks, from the *Daily News*, was sitting in the passenger seat and had the window down.

"Quick!" he repeated.

Miles and I scrambled to our feet and made a mad dash for the car. Miles got there first and jumped through the window, on top of Jimmy, leaving exactly zero room for me to squeeze in.

I could see that he was desperately trying to slither inside and make some space, but I was stuck on the outside. A giddy kind of panic tore through me as I wheeled around to face the mob of zompires that was advancing on me.

Time slowed down. Even the raindrops slowed down. I could almost count the spider blossoms on Creed's teeth, scurrying in and out between them and along her gums. Behind her, ten other zompires snarled at me, baring their own thorny fangs.

Then Creed lunged. Her hands latched on to my shoulders like vice grips, and she leaned in. Sadly, I was a deer in headlights, frozen and helpless, and for the briefest of moments, my short life flashed in front of my eyes. It was just like a scene you'd see in a sappy movie. Strange memories. A birthday with Lilith when I sat on her cake. Riding a roller coaster at Disneyland with Johnny. My mom putting a bandage on a scraped knee. My dad hugging me goodnight.

Luckily, Jimmy threw an uppercut under my arm that connected with Creed's jaw. Her mouth snapped shut with a sloppy click, bringing me out of my trance, and I followed his uppercut with a hard punch to her gut. Her hands fell off my shoulders, and she stumbled back a step.

"Get *in*!" Jimmy cried.

I whirled around and saw that Miles was halfway into the backseat, so I dove in toward Jimmy's feet. As I did, one of the zompires, possibly Creed, grabbed on to the back of my T-shirt.

In horror movies, there's always that one poor sap who gets dragged into a seething mob of monsters while his friends look on. I kind of always pictured myself more as the smart-alecky hero, rather than the bit-part player who gets eaten halfway through the show, but I had a sinking feeling I was about to become that minor player. I heard my shirt rip a little and hooked my fingers under the front of the seat.

"Get off him!" Jimmy Brooks growled, as the car's engine revved.

Elizabeth floored it, and the tires screeched. Someone else out there latched on to one of my legs. I had a vision of them crunching down on it, and I kicked both legs desperately just as the car shot forward, knocking them away.

My shirt stretched, and there was another rip as the seams around my neck started to give out. Whoever had the other end wasn't letting go, even though we were already flying down Beech Street. The part of the collar that hadn't ripped yet was digging into my neck, and I was slowly being dragged out of the window.

"Faster!" I croaked hoarsely. I could barely breathe anymore, and my grip on the seat was loosening.

Elizabeth shifted gears again. The collar dug even deeper. I closed my eyes. I heard another rip, like a short but powerful fart, and then another.

I groaned. Black dots were popping up in front of me. I was going to pass out.

"Hold on!" Elizabeth yelled. "We're turning!"

Tires squealed so suddenly to the left, I thought the car

was going to roll over. I lost my grip on the bottom of the seat and jolted backward a few inches. Jimmy grabbed on to me. "I got you," he said.

In my mind's eye, I imagined my shirt stretched out twenty or thirty feet behind us, with some determined zompire being dragged along the wet asphalt.

"Hold on!" Elizabeth screamed again, as I grabbed on to the drink console.

For an instant, I thought I was going to lose my grip, but then my shirt whipped off of me with hardly a sound, leaving only the collar, which hung around my neck like an enormous cloth necklace.

"I'm in," I gasped, finally pulling my legs inside and clambering into the back with Miles.

"Hold on," Elizabeth said, as we went around a curve in the road.

"What now?" Jimmy asked.

"To the highway," Miles said.

Rain was pelting in through the open window, splattering my face and chest. Jimmy rolled it up as Elizabeth swerved around another bend in the road.

"We need to go back to the inn," I said.

"No, no, no, no," Miles said. "We can't. We barely made it off of Beech Street. I know you want to save your mom, but our first priority should be to get out of Rolling Hills and alert the authorities immediately. We've got a car full of witnesses now, who will verify the existence of a deadly infection spreading through this town."

"Just drop me off," I said. "I'll get her, and we'll make it out of here on our own."

"I don't think that's a good idea," Jimmy said, but Elizabeth was slowing down.

"I understand if you don't want to stick around. Just drive me back to the inn, and you can run for the hills ... or out of the hills, I guess."

Elizabeth pulled over to the side. She was practically hyperventilating, and her arms were trembling as she gripped the steering wheel with white knuckles. I didn't know what street we were on, but it was lined with big old houses just like all the other side streets in Rolling Hills.

"My dad ..." Elizabeth said, her voice shaking. "He was out there with them. What's wrong with him?"

"Ah, well ..." I started, not really knowing how I could explain this. Her eyes were welling up with tears, and then Miles cut in.

"We're dealing with an infection," Miles said matter-of-factly. "It appears to be caused by a parasitic organism that attacks the brain ..."

Elizabeth started crying, and I racked my brain for something to say that would make her feel better, but I was coming up empty. There's just no way to put a silver lining on a mind-altering parasitic plague.

"I can't believe I didn't notice it," Jimmy said. "I was so worried about getting all those stupid graduation announcements in the paper that I didn't notice a zombie outbreak in my own town."

"They're not zombies," Miles said.

"Vampires?" Jimmy asked.

"Is my dad a vampire?" Elizabeth asked, her voice rising.

"No," Miles said quickly. "They just exhibit some of the behaviors that are typically associated with vampirism, like heightened motor skills, increased strength and speed, telepathic communication, and they have fangs. But I wouldn't classify them as vampires, not in the classical sense."

"Why are they so fast?" Jimmy asked, looking back at Miles.

"I don't know for sure, but I think the invading organism may shut down the body's normal pain responses. So, it drives the host far beyond any normal human limits. It may also tap into regions of the brain that we don't normally use, or don't know how to use properly. But that doesn't matter right now. We're dealing with an epidemic here, people! A real infection that's hurting real people and we have to do something about it! We have to get out of town and tell someone in a position of authority so it doesn't spread beyond the borders of Rolling Hills."

"Winehurst," I said, "take me back to the inn. Just drop me off, then you guys can make a run for ... what's the nearest town?"

"Hillsboro," she said.

"Right, make a run for Hillsboro. My mom might not be infected yet, and I'm not a hundred percent certain about Lilith. If Lilith is okay, there's a good chance my mom will be okay. I've got to try."

"Listen, Charlie, my mom's out there, too," Miles said, "but we can't risk getting caught. We have to make it to Hillsboro and spread the word."

"There might be others," I said. "And besides, if we get my mom, we can pick up the truck, then we can go to your place and pick up your mom, too. We could all get out of town together. Please, Winehurst."

"The sooner we get word out about this outbreak," Miles said, talking to Elizabeth, "the sooner they might be able to help the people who are infected, including your dad."

"I can walk," I said. "I just don't want to leave her up there."

Elizabeth sighed and wiped her eyes. "Okay, Charlie. I'll take you back, but you have to promise me one thing: if she's infected, we just leave. You're not going to try to capture her or anything."

"If she's infected, I wouldn't have a prayer against her anyway. I'll just walk away ... actually, I'll probably have to run."

"I'll go with you," Jimmy said. "Man, when I run this story, I could land a big-time job, maybe the *New York Times*!"

Miles sighed. "I'm really going to regret this when I'm completely surrounded and about to become one of the infected, but fine, okay, I'm in."

"All right then," Elizabeth said and pulled a U-turn. "We're going back to Elm Street."

Sunday, 9:30 p.m.

I was terrified there would be another mob of zompires waiting for us by the Baxter place, but the road was clear, and the Baxters' house looked as normal as ever. Although, I did make a mental note that their car was not in the driveway.

As we approached the inn, Miles said, "I don't think we should park in the driveway. They'll see us coming, and it's way too easy to get boxed in."

"It's going to make for a long run," Jimmy said, "if we're in a rush coming out."

"They're going to be moving fast," I said, but Elizabeth was already pulling onto the side of the road, about fifty yards from the inn's driveway.

"Jimmy, Miles, let's move," I said, as the car came to a stop. "Winehurst, we'll be back ASAP."

"I'm not staying in the car by myself," Elizabeth said.

"Someone's got to stay in the car," Miles said as Jimmy climbed out. "If things get messy, and we can't get back, or if we get infected, then one of us has to get out of town and spread the word."

"It's going to be dangerous," I said. "You're probably better off if —"

"I stay behind?" she said sharply. "Listen to me, Choke, I'm not going to bother telling you all the ins and outs of how I arrived on Beech Street and saved your spoiled hiney, but it wasn't because I'm not capable of dealing with dangerous situations."

"She's right about that," Jimmy said, pulling the seat forward so that Miles and I could get out. "I'd still be trapped inside The Opal with about thirty other people if it weren't for her."

"It was a stupid thing to say," I said, sliding out. "We all go inside together. Besides, people are always splitting up in horror movies, and it never works out. It will be better this way."

"This is the real world, Charlie," Miles said, getting out, too, "and we're dealing with a real outbreak of a real infection. I think someone needs to stay behind."

"You can hang back if you want," I said.

Miles hesitated, glancing from me to the car and then back at me. "No, you'll need my expertise. I've trained for this type of situation."

"I'll leave the keys on the seat," Elizabeth said.

"Good idea," Miles said. "I seriously doubt we're all going to make it back."

"That's uplifting," I said.

"I'm just being realistic."

"Miles Van Helsing, Realist," I said.

Jimmy laughed, and the sound cut through the night.

"Miles might be right, though. Look, this is my family. You don't have to do this," I said, scanning the road. It was pitch-black all around us. "Maybe you should just drop me off and get to Hillsboro."

"Excellent idea," Miles said.

"No," Elizabeth snapped. "We're a team now — we'll stick together."

"Agreed," Jimmy said. "If we can escape from them once, we can escape from them again."

"Don't count on it," Miles muttered, but he didn't get back in the car.

"Since we're a team, I don't suppose you've got an extra shirt in the trunk?" I asked Elizabeth, pointing at my stretched-out shirt collar. "Although I like the ventilation, I prefer a shirt with a little more ... um, material."

"I think I might have a bikini top in there," she said.

"Nah, I don't think that's the right look for me."

"What's the plan? Are we just going to walk through the front door?" Jimmy asked, as we started down the road.

"I think we should approach the house through the woods," Miles said. "And use the back door as our entry point."

"Then what?" Elizabeth asked, following Miles across the street and into the woods.

Sunday, 9:35 p.m.

We huddled together, staring out of the trees. The lights were all off inside the inn, and the moon was stuck behind all those rain clouds, so it was shockingly dark. I could still make out Jake's pickup, though, which was parked in front of Mom's truck.

"That's Jake's truck," I whispered.

"Who?" Jimmy asked.

"Jake Steel, he's helping us out with the renovations. He has four guys in his work crew, and they're all infected. Five, with Johnny," I said. "Six, if Lilith is infected, too."

"That's not good," Jimmy muttered.

"Stick together," Miles whispered and started out of the trees.

I followed him, with Elizabeth and Jimmy right behind me. We all ran, hunched over, as if getting a little closer to the ground would actually make us harder to see. It's possible it worked, though, because we reached the back door without anyone leaping out at us. But I wasn't taking anything for granted since they might all be patiently waiting for us to come inside.

"It's unlocked," Miles said, opening the door. He was about to go in when I grabbed his arm.

"Let me go in first," I whispered, tiptoeing past him.

The shabby little TV room looked no different from when we'd gone in with Hal on Friday night, but the house reeked of fresh paint. Whatever had happened here today, they'd at least started to paint the place.

"Stay sharp," I said. It was a ridiculous thing to say, but I had to say something, or my mind was going to crack under the pressure.

The others followed me in, trying to step lightly, but no matter how carefully we walked, the hardwood floor creaked. I was grateful for the rain pelting against the roof, which was loud enough to mask some of the creaking and squeaking. Those were the only sounds in the place. Unless you counted the sound of my heart hammering against my ribs. My senses were so heightened from fear and paranoia at that point, I was pretty sure I could hear my fingernails growing.

We crept across the room, inching along, toward the door in the far corner, which was open. I peeked into the dining room and saw that it was empty, except for the chairs and table, which were still covered by white sheets.

"Clear," I whispered, and we snuck into the dining room, hugging the wall.

The sitting room floor was covered in sheets, and paint cans were stacked in the corner.

"Stay here," I said. "I'll check across the hall."

I crept through the sitting room and poked my head into the foyer. I couldn't see anyone in the drawing room, the hallway, on the stairs or on the upstairs landing, but most of the drawing room was hidden from view, and it was pretty dark, so if someone was hiding, I might not see them. For all I knew, Johnny and Jake's men could be lurking in there with the antique dolls, waiting to pounce. But, I told myself, they could also be out for the night, busy infecting people other than my mom.

I slunk back to the dining room. "I think the coast is clear," I whispered.

"You think? Aren't you positive?" Jimmy asked. He was twitching around like he'd lost control of his body. "I'm not getting a good vibe, Charlie."

"The coast is clear," I repeated. I couldn't think of anything else to say and watching Jimmy twitch around was making me even edgier, which meant that on a nervousness scale of 1 to 10, I was now hovering at about a 53.

"Let's keep going," Elizabeth said. She and Miles looked calm by contrast, as if they'd resigned themselves to getting caught.

"Okay," I said, and we all creaked our way into the foyer.

"Upstairs?" Miles asked.

I nodded.

I'd just put my foot on the first step, with the others

crowding around behind me, when the front door burst open. I'd been coiled up so tightly I sprang at least four feet into the air and spun around, a silent scream caught in my throat. Jimmy collapsed on the ground, scratching at the wall, while Miles and Elizabeth grabbed on to each other. Elizabeth stayed perfectly quiet, but Miles cried out something that sounded like "Jangza!"

All that happened before I could even register that it was Lilith standing in the doorway. She was dressed in some kind of ninja costume, minus the mask. Instead, she'd streaked her face with black war paint and was carrying a five-foot-long wooden staff.

"They followed you here," she growled, walking into the foyer.

"W-W-Where's Mom?" I stuttered, now twitching myself. Although I was better off than Jimmy, who was shaking on the stairs so vigorously I thought he might be having a seizure.

"Safe — until now," Lilith said, and then Lennox rumbled through the door behind her.

Lilith swirled around and jabbed him in the nose with the staff, stopping him in his tracks. She twirled the staff in her hands like a baton and then swung it like a baseball bat at his knees, sweeping his legs out from under him.

"Go down to the cellar and out the back," she said and tossed me the key for the cellar door. Hamish Frog came through the front door next. Lilith tried to whack him with the staff, but he caught it with his hand, so she followed up with a snapping front kick to his privates.

Hamish didn't cry out, but he went down, releasing the staff.

"Move it!" Lilith screamed.

"We should listen to her," Elizabeth said.

"Yeah," I said and took one last look up the stairs, before corralling everyone down the hall, toward the kitchen.

"Go! Go! Go!" I cried, pushing Miles and Elizabeth along in front of me. Jimmy was practically running up my back as we sprinted toward the kitchen.

As we ran past the ancient refrigerator, I glanced over my shoulder. Lilith was holding her own against two more zompires that had wandered inside, but then Dutton limped out of the sitting room, behind her.

"Lilith, look out!" I cried.

She whipped around, without looking, and nailed Dutton with a roundhouse kick to his square jaw. He crashed into the wall and slumped to the floor.

"She's amazing," Miles said, pulling me away.

"Yeah," I said, crossing the kitchen and throwing open the door to the cellar.

"Watch the stairs," I said, as Elizabeth went in, followed by Miles.

"Hurry, Jimmy," I said, holding the door open, but he was backing away.

"I can't go down there," he stammered. "That's where people go to die! The monsters always catch you in the basement! I'll find somewhere to hide up here."

"Are you crazy? They'll find you!"

"I can't!" he screamed, still twitching all over. "Just go!"

In the foyer I heard Lilith scream out, "Hee-ya!," and then the sound of feet, lots of feet, were storming down the hallway. An instant later, Baxter appeared down the hall, snarling. He was followed by Balic and the indestructible Dutton, who had blood streaming out of his now crooked nose.

"Go!" Jimmy cried, and then he made a break for the pantry door at the other end of the kitchen.

It was Miles who pulled me in and slammed the door shut. It got really, really dark, really, really fast, and I felt my way down the stairs before bumping into Elizabeth.

"Where are we going?" she said and clicked her phone on. The light from the display created a small bubble of visibility.

"Move, move, move!" Miles said, coming down the stairs.

"Go straight!" I cried, and we hustled along the hallway.

The stink of moldy soil was all around me. The walls were so close together I was grazing my shoulders along the cold stones, and I had to hunch forward or I'd hit my head on the ceiling. I couldn't help thinking that Jimmy might have been right, maybe this is where they wanted us to go.

"There's a left turn coming up," I said.

An instant later, Elizabeth made the turn.

"Go straight until we get to a door," I said, feeling the weight of the key in my hand.

"I can hear them! They're coming through the door," Miles hissed from behind me. "Move it!"

We darted down the dank corridor together. I could hear the footsteps marching down the stairs, streaming into the cellar behind us.

"It's close," I said, feeling a fresh and almost overwhelming wave of panic and terror sweep through me. We were in a giant grave, and I didn't even know what had happened to Lilith or Mom. All I could do was keep moving.

"The key," Elizabeth said, stopping so suddenly I bumped into her. "The key," she repeated, and I tried to give it to her, but I fumbled and it fell onto the ground.

She dropped to her knees and scanned around with her phone.

"Got it!" she cried, as Miles bumped into me.

"Hurry, hurry, hurry," he said, but we didn't need the reminder. We could all hear their footsteps closing in.

I don't know if I would have been capable of putting the key in the lock, my hands were shaking so much, but Elizabeth managed to do it.

On the way through, I pulled the key back out of the lock and Miles slammed the door shut. I thrust the key at Elizabeth, being extra careful not to drop it this time.

"You can lock it from this side, too," I said. "I'm too shaky."

"Done," Elizabeth said, and a moment later someone slammed into the other side. Dust from the ceiling snowed onto my head.

"Now what?" Miles asked. "I don't think the door will hold for long."

I eased my way toward the back of the room. In the hall, someone delivered another blow to the door, and I heard the wood splinter and crack.

Miles groaned.

"The back door is this way ... I think," I said. I could smell the paint, mixing with the scent of damp soil and old boxes. There was another violent cracking of wood, and then I stepped on something that creaked under me. I looked down and saw a thin line of light. It was so faint I thought I might be imagining it. That's when I remembered the trapdoor.

Someone crashed into the door again, and a splintering, splitting sound cut through the darkness.

"They're almost in!" Miles cried.

I got down on my hands and knees and felt for the handle that I knew was in the middle of the door.

"This way, quick!" I hissed, and found the handle. "Quick!"

"Where are you?" Elizabeth said and then she kneed me on the side of the head. "Sorry."

"I'm okay. Move back a bit," I said. I hoisted the door open.

There was another splintering crack from the hallway door, but I barely noticed it. My attention was fixed on a square concrete shaft that went straight down for about twenty feet. A metal ladder ran along one side. On the other side, about halfway down, a light was attached to the wall, emitting a soft glow. At the bottom of that shaft, on the wall between the ladder and the light, there was a metal door.

Miles cried, "They're coming in!"

"Miles!" Elizabeth called. "We're over here!"

Another crack and I heard a metallic popping sound, and then Miles screamed.

"Miles!" I called, as Elizabeth was starting down the ladder.

"Quick, it's our only chance," she said, looking up at me.

"Run!" Miles screamed, and I heard wild scuffling through the darkness.

Footsteps rushed toward me as I started down the ladder. I grabbed the edge of the trapdoor and pulled it shut, but it swung back open immediately, and Johnny's face appeared out of the darkness. Shocked, I lost my footing and then my grip on the ladder. I fell for a bit, flailing my arms, before I managed to grab hold of the ladder again. I looked back up. Johnny was staring down at me, his face completely devoid of any feeling, or of any recognition at all. He looked like a person who'd died with their eyes open. Just seeing him like that made my insides turn to ice — then his lips parted in a snarl, revealing a mouthful of fangs.

Elizabeth screamed, then I screamed, and Johnny started climbing down the ladder. I decided to forget about using the rungs and just slid down the rest of the way, landing beside Elizabeth an instant later. She was frantically trying to twist the thick metal handle on the door up or down, but it wouldn't budge.

"It's locked!" she cried.

I looked up. Johnny was halfway down, and now Baxter was looking down at us from the top.

I probably would have just stood there and waited like a cornered rabbit until Johnny bit me, but there was a hiss behind us, and suddenly the metal door swung open. Standing in the doorway, holding his shotgun, was Uncle Hal. He was sporting a plush red bathrobe and silky-looking red pajamas. He was clean-shaven and, apart from the curly, wild hair, generally looked a lot less crazy than the first time we'd met.

"Get in," he grumbled.

Elizabeth didn't hesitate. She plowed through the door, which looked like it was about a foot thick. I piled in after her, just as Johnny dropped down from the ladder, landing right behind me.

"Back!" Hal commanded and hit Johnny in the face with the butt of his gun. Johnny fell backward, his movie-star nose spouting blood, and Hal pushed the door shut. It closed with another hiss, and then he grabbed on to a steering-wheel-sized disk on the inside of the door. He spun it around, and a bolt (it sounded like a really big bolt) thudded into place. Above the door, a green light went out, and a red light flicked on.

"You shouldn't be out running around this late at night," he said, turning to us. "And for Pete's sake, Charlie, where's your shirt? There's a young lady present."

"Somebody took it from me ..." I said, looking around in disbelief. We were inside some kind of bunker, about the size of a small apartment, but Hal had it decorated like a ritzy mansion from the 1950s. There were ornate Persian rugs on the floor, dark wooden tables and chairs here and there, a cushy sofa, a huge desk covered in papers, a large dresser and an old-fashioned record player. The tiny kitchen area had a sink, a microwave and a small stovetop. In the back corner of the room were two sets of bunk beds, each with a red sleeping bag rolled out.

"We'll have to rectify that," he said, putting the shotgun down by the door and strolling toward us. "But first, I think introductions are in order."

"I'm ... I'm ..." Elizabeth started, looking shocked.

"This is Elizabeth Opal," I said.

"I thought so," Hal said and put his hands together, like he was saying a prayer, and bowed slightly. "You look like your mother."

"You knew my mother?"

"Yes, but not very well," he said. Not only did he not look half as crazy as before, but he also wasn't acting half as crazy. And he could hear.

"You can hear," I said.

"I've got my hearing aids in," he said, pointing at his ears. "They don't bother me down here — not as much interference, I guess. Plus, I can't listen to my music without them," he added, walking over to the record player beside his desk and flicking up a switch. Jazz music whirled on, slow and slurry at first, but gradually spinning into normal speed.

"My father was a big jazz fan," he said. "It keeps me company."

"How long have you been staying down here, Uncle Hal?" I asked, glancing at the door, expecting Johnny and the rest of them to burst in at any minute despite the thick metal door.

"When your mother decided she was going to make the place into a gard-darned bed-and-breakfast, or whatever she's doing, I started moving some of my things down. When Baxter brought back that package and went loopy — well, I decided to make it my permanent home."

"Whoa, back up a second," I said. "You knew about Baxter?"

"I knew something bad was going to come of all his digging around sooner or later."

"They can't get in, can they?" Elizabeth asked, glancing nervously at the door.

"Miss Opal, this bomb shelter was constructed in 1955, and it was built to withstand an atomic blast. I would be very, very surprised if they could get inside."

"What are we going to do?" I asked. "Do you have a phone, a computer, anything we can use to get in touch with someone outside to tell them what's going on?"

"Afraid not. My father built this retreat so the family could survive a war, not surf the web. Plus, you can't get any reception down here."

"He's right," Elizabeth said, showing me her phone.

"Well, we have to do something. Mom and Lilith are still up there."

"I'll tell you what you can do. You can have a hot shower," Hal said. "You darned well need one — you're filthy. There's a washroom back there," he added, pointing behind a wooden divider in the far corner, opposite the bunk beds.

"A hot shower? You've got to be kidding me, Uncle Hal! We don't have time for hot showers. There's a freaking invasion of the zompires happening out there. They've got Johnny, and Mom and Lilith might be next."

"And Miles, probably," Elizabeth muttered.

"Yeah, and Miles," I said, feeling sick that he hadn't made it down here with us. "We've got to do something to help them!"

"Come with me," Hal said, waving me over to the door.

For a second, I thought he was going to kick me out, and I have to admit I momentarily regretted all that hero talk. But instead of opening the door, he slid open a shoebox-sized panel beside the door, revealing a small screen. It showed the inside of the concrete tunnel outside. Johnny and Baxter were taking turns crashing into the door.

"Now tell me, kid — do you want me to open up the door and send you outside, or are you going to take some time to clean up and figure things out? By the time you're done washing up, those two yahoos might actually be gone."

"He's got a point, Charlie," Elizabeth said. She was standing behind us, looking at the screen over my shoulder. Her hair was a tangled mess, her face was smudged with dirt and she had about a half dozen scratches running across each arm. "We need rest and some time to think. Just an hour or so."

"Listen to the girl, kid," Hal said, sliding the panel shut.

"All right, fine. But tell me this, Uncle Hal — how do you

have a functioning shower down here? The plumbing in the inn is shot. I haven't been able to shower for days."

"Near the end of his life, my father became obsessed with the idea that nuclear war was going to erupt at any moment. So, he spent what was left of his fortune upgrading this bunker. One of the improvements he made was connecting the plumbing system in here to the well, using a state-of-the-art filtration system, just to make sure we didn't end up drinking contaminated water," he said, strolling toward the back of the bunker. "Long story short, kid, the bunker siphons water from the same well as the house. I guess that might have been useful information for your mom and the plumbers."

"Probably," I said, stepping behind the wooden divider. The shower stall was just a small square tub, about three feet deep, with a showerhead on a hose attached to the side.

"We don't have any water issues down here, so take your time. Of course, if you want to be a gentleman, Charlie, you could let Miss Opal go first."

"No, that's okay, Charlie," Elizabeth said.

"No, no, he's right," I said. "Besides, it will give me more time to gallivant around without my shirt on."

"I'll grab you some new clothes," Hal said. "When they built the bunker, they stocked it with about fifty uniforms."

"That sounds fine," she said.

Hal strolled over to the large dresser, which stood against the wall a few feet from the bunk beds, and opened a bottom drawer. It was stuffed with sealed bags of orange uniforms.

"They're vacuum-packed, so they're as fresh as they were in 1955," he said, pulling out a bag from the bottom. "A small should do for Miss Opal, and a large for you," he added and tossed me one of the bags.

Then he opened the dresser and grabbed one of five or six thick white towels that were stacked on one of the shelves. I noticed the other shelves were stuffed with his own clothes. There was even a section where he had a dozen or so dress shirts hanging.

"You don't go in for orange jumpsuits?" I asked.

"I had time to pack," he said, brushing past me.

"Miss Opal, I'm going to toss over your uniform and towel," he called from our side of the divider. Elizabeth had already started the shower, and I could see steam rising toward the ceiling.

"Okay," she called back.

Hal reached over the divider and dropped the towel and uniform bag, then he turned back to me. "Let me show you something, Charlie."

I followed him over to the large desk, which was about halfway to the front of the room and covered in newspapers and notebooks.

"I'm writing my memoirs," he said, sweeping his hand over the papers. "So I've been looking at old photos." He pulled open a side drawer and removed a thick file folder. "I think you'll find this one interesting."

He handed me a photo of a group of kids, about my age, standing on the front porch of the inn. There was a *Happy Birthday!* banner hanging above them and they were all dressed in shorts and T-shirts. I spotted my mom almost right away, but it was the kid standing next to her that made my jaw drop.

"I knew you'd find that interesting," Hal said, chuckling.

I pulled the photo up to my face for a closer look, but that didn't make what I was seeing any less bewildering. There, standing on the porch beside my mom, in a picture that was probably taken about thirty-five years ago, was me.

"That's me," Hal said, tapping my doppelgänger.

I looked at Hal, then at the photo, then back at Hal.

"You've got all this to look forward to, kid," he said, grinning with that crazy look again.

"That's you?" I said.

"The rest of the family has the blond hair, blue eyes, square-jaw genes. You and me, Charlie, we've got the curly hair, brown eyes, slightly crazy genes. I think we get them from my great-great-uncle Max. He tried to sail around the world — only from north to south instead of east to west. He didn't make it."

"We're twins," I mumbled.

He nodded. "We're family, kid. We're not that different, and we need to stick together. I'm looking out for you — you're just going to have to trust me on that."

Elizabeth cut in before I could answer. "How do I look?" she asked, stepping out from behind the wooden divider.

I was expecting the orange uniforms Hal had given us to be like coveralls, kind of loose and baggy, but they were more like tights. They reminded me of Lilith's Uber-Jams.

"You kind of look like a carrot, or a very thin pumpkin, Winehurst."

"Always the charmer," she said.

"Let's see how *you* look in one of those, smart guy," Hal said. "And grab a towel out of the dresser on your way by."

I took a long, hot shower. It was hard to enjoy, considering every time I closed my eyes I saw little red spiders floating around. Plus, I couldn't get Johnny's thousand-yard stare out of my mind. It was all too horrible to be real — it couldn't be real. I couldn't accept it. There had to be a cure, and we had to get out of here to find it. Lilith and Mom were out there somewhere. The only consolation I could take away from that was that if I had to pick any one person in the universe to help Mom survive, it would be Lilith.

When I was done with the shower, I put on my I-survived-an-atomic-blast uniform. I felt like Superman, only without the cape, bulging muscles or any superpowers that might make wearing a skintight outfit acceptable. The only bonus was that it came with padded booties.

"I don't suppose you've got an extra-large one of these uniforms, Uncle Hal?" I called from behind the divider. "Or an extra-extra-large?"

"Afraid not," he said.

"Maybe I could borrow some of your clothes?" I said.

"Not going to happen."

"Just come out, Charlie," Elizabeth said. "Hal's made us tea and oatmeal."

"You might want to look away if you're eating," I said and ventured out.

Elizabeth froze, holding a spoonful of oatmeal about halfway to her mouth. Hal, who was looking over the edge of a mug that he was sipping out of, did the same.

"I warned you," I said.

Hal lowered the mug. Elizabeth crammed the spoon into her mouth and tried not to laugh, but couldn't stop herself.

"Go ahead, laugh, but I think you should know I've always been good at holding a grudge, and you two are going down on my list of people who deserve to be grudged, and for a long time!"

"Sorry," Elizabeth sputtered. "It's just that you look so ... well ... so ..."

"Ridiculous," Hal chimed in.

"Yes, but apparently I'd fit right in if this were 1955 and we were living down here after a nuclear blast," I said, strolling over to a chair beside Elizabeth and sitting down. "And I'd also like to note that these booties are pretty comfortable."

"Here," Hal said, thrusting a bowl of steaming oatmeal into my hands. "Eat up."

I tasted a spoonful. It was pretty darned good, and I was starving, so I dug in. Elizabeth must have been hungry, too, because we sat in silence for a few minutes, gorging ourselves on the stuff. When I was done, Hal handed me a mug full of tea. I gulped down a few mouthfuls and sat back, feeling warm and full and comfortable — too comfortable, considering my sister and mother were out there, fighting for their lives. Or their brains at the very least.

I looked at Elizabeth and then at Hal. "We have to talk about getting out of here and helping Lilith and my mom, and Johnny, your dad, Miles ... the whole flipping town if we can!"

"We should get the word out, too, to anyone who will listen, before this thing spreads to other places," Elizabeth added.

"There'll be time for that later," Hal said.

"No. There's no time," I said. "This is an emergency, Uncle Hal. We have to do something now." I tried to stand up, but my legs went rubbery, and I fell back into the chair.

"I feel sleepy," Elizabeth said, her words slurring together a little.

"Me, too," I said, and the room tilted.

"Come on," Hal said, grabbing me under my arms and hoisting me out of the chair. "I'm not going to let you go out there and get yourself hurt just because you think you need to be some kind of hero. The world doesn't want heroes, Charlie. You'll learn that eventually."

"Did you put something in our food?" I mumbled.

"I have a hard time sleeping sometimes," he said, guiding me toward the bunk beds. "The doc gives me sleeping pills. I just sprinkled a few granules into your oatmeal. It's nothing serious, and in the morning, you'll be able to think straight. Then you'll see I was right about playing it safe."

"That isn't right," I muttered, and he dumped me into one of the beds.

Hal smiled down at me, and then I passed out.

Monday, 3:30 a.m.

I woke up in the dark, to a voice whispering in my ear, "Wake up, Charlie."

I couldn't place it.

"Wake up," it hissed.

I couldn't figure out where I was. In my room at Choke? Hawaii? No ... the inn?

"Charlie, wake up," the voice whispered. "Please, wake up."

Then it hit me. I was in the bunker; Hal had drugged us. Us ...

Elizabeth was with me.

My eyes popped open. A hand shot over my mouth, and Elizabeth's face appeared inches from mine.

"*Shh,*" she said, holding a finger in front of her lips. "He's asleep."

I gave her the okay sign, and she moved her hand off of my mouth. "What time is it?" I whispered.

"Three thirty in the morning." She pointed at a digital clock mounted on the wall. The numbers were green and sending a faint glow out into the room. It was the only light in the place.

"Where is he?"

She pointed toward the sofa, and I saw him splayed out, still wearing his bathrobe.

"We can't stay here," she said. "I think he's gone crazy."

"Oh, he's definitely gone crazy," I whispered, and eased my way up and into a sitting position on the side of the bed. I added *don't end up hiding in a bunker when you get older* to my mental to-do list. Hal and I might have a few genes in common, but that didn't mean my life had to follow the same path to Crazy Town.

"We need to go now," she said, standing up slowly.

I got up, too, and followed her across the room, toward the door. We inched our way along, being careful not to run into anything.

We were between the sofa and the kitchen area when about a dozen pots and pans came crashing to the ground all around us.

"Darn!" Elizabeth hissed, and a flashlight flicked on.

"I thought you might try something like this," Hal said, sitting up and pointing the light into our eyes.

"We just want to go, Uncle Hal."

"What?" he said. "What did you say?"

"We want to leave."

"Huh? You'll have to speak up. I don't have my hearing aids in," he said, getting up off the sofa.

"He can't hear a thing without those hearing aids," I whispered to Elizabeth. "Get behind him."

She nodded and drifted back toward the beds.

"I left them on my desk," Hal grumbled.

While he got up and headed for the desk, I quickly slipped around the sofa.

"Not so fast, kiddo," he said, and I heard a click. "I've

got a flashlight in one hand and my shotgun in the other. Like I said before, making you stay put is for your own good."

"Hal, don't do anything crazy. Please, listen to me," I pleaded.

"Huh? What?"

"Listen!" I screamed. "Mom and Lilith are out there! I need to see if they're okay!"

"That's what I've been saying, kid — we'll wait until the day," he said. "Then you'll see what I'm talking about."

Hal was at the desk now and put his flashlight down, although he kept it aimed straight at me. I could hear him patting around for his hearing aids.

"No! We need to help Mom! And Lilith! And everyone else for that matter!"

"Here they are," he said.

With the flashlight blazing in my direction, I couldn't see Elizabeth. I could only hope she was behind Uncle Hal and could get the drop on him.

"I don't want to stay down here, hiding like a chicken!"

"You don't have to yell," Hal said. "I can hear you. I've got my hearing aids in. Now where's the girl?"

"Right here," I heard Elizabeth say, and then there was a loud clanging sound, like two pots being bashed together.

That's when three things happened, almost all at once: Hal screamed in pain, the flashlight dropped and the gun went off.

I threw myself at Hal. We crashed onto the floor, the gun clattering away.

"My ears," he roared, thrashing his way out from under me and getting back up onto his feet. "She's deafened me!"

I scrambled after him and jumped onto his back. Amazingly, he stayed up, with me hanging on to him, piggyback style. I bucked and twisted, trying to bring him down.

"Get off!" he grunted, stumbling around.

"Let us leave!" I shouted, straight into his right ear.

"Gard-darn it, kid, it's not safe out there!" he cried, whirling around and around in the dark, bumping into things, kicking pots, until Elizabeth rushed over and rammed us from the side.

"Raah!" Hal cried, as we sidestepped into the record player. The whole thing toppled over, crashing to the ground beside us.

We hit the concrete floor hard, with me on the bottom, and all the air exited my body. Hal rolled off of me, and I wheezed violently, trying to breathe.

"Are you okay, Charlie?" Elizabeth asked, rushing over.

I tried to answer, but couldn't. I gasped and struggled to my knees.

"What's wrong?" Elizabeth pleaded, helping me stand up.

I gulped in air and nodded. "I'm okay," I squeaked.

Hal didn't get up. He was kneeling beside the record player, which had broken into two big pieces. Wires were hanging out, and a few of the internal pieces were now external pieces.

"How could you?" he moaned. "You killed my music, you maniacs!"

"You shot at us," I said weakly.

"The music," he grumbled, trying to fit the two pieces of the record player back together.

"Come on, Charlie," Elizabeth said, grabbing Hal's shotgun, which he seemed to have forgotten. "Let's go."

She handed me the gun and held out her phone in front of us to light our way with the display.

"My music," Hal muttered mournfully. "How am I going to listen to it now?"

Elizabeth and I rushed to the door and I slid open the panel, revealing the video monitor. There was no sign of Baxter or Johnny outside.

"They're gone," Elizabeth said.

"Yeah, but how far did they go?"

"There's only one way to find out," she said and grabbed on to the disk in the middle of the door.

That's when Hal came looming out of the darkness, like a monster coming back to life. "Do not open that door!" he roared.

I wasn't willing to shoot Hal, so I swung the gun in front of me like a baseball bat, to ward him off.

"Stay back, Uncle Hal! We're leaving!"

"You can't leave!" he shouted. "They're out there, kid, and they'll get you. Don't you see, I'm trying to keep you safe! There's no need to risk your life! Just stay down here with me until this all blows over."

"It's not going to blow over!" I said. "And Mom's out there, and Lilith — I've got to try to help them."

"Don't try to be a hero, kid," Hal said. "Believe me, it's not worth it. You just end up by yourself."

"I've got to try," I said, and I heard Elizabeth turn the disk. An instant later, the bolt clicked, and the light above the door changed from red to green.

"I'm taking the gun," I said, as Elizabeth pulled the door open.

"I didn't mean to shoot, kid," Hal said. "That was an accident."

"Just the same, I'd like to hang on to it. And when all this blows over, I'll buy you a new record player," I said as we stepped out of the bunker and into the concrete shaft. It was still empty, and the trapdoor at the top of the ladder was still open. Beyond it was only darkness.

"Don't be a hero," Hal repeated weakly, and he stepped forward and pushed the door shut. It closed with a hiss.

"What now?" Elizabeth whispered.

"I hate to say it, Winehurst, but I think the smartest thing to do is get out of town as fast as possible. There's no way we can risk trying to find my mom, or anyone else, and the sooner we get help for your dad and Johnny, the sooner they'll be back to normal."

"I'm not sure anyone's going to be able to help my dad and Johnny," she said.

"We have to try," I said. "Otherwise we may as well stay holed up in that bunker. Is that what you want to do?"

"I don't think he'd let us back in," she said.

"Which means there's only one way to go now ..." I said. "Up."

She nodded. "If we can get to my car, we might have a chance."

"I'll lead the way to the cellar door," I said, grabbing on to the ladder. "If it's locked, I'll try to blast it open with the shotgun."

"And if we can't get it open?" she asked, starting up behind me.

"Then we'll have to go upstairs and through the front door."

She didn't say anything else and neither did I. We both knew going upstairs and through the front door would probably be the end of our story. Heck, I had a feeling that popping my head out of the trapdoor and into the cellar was probably going to be the end of the line for Charles Harker. But I didn't have a choice, so when I got to the top, I just scrambled up and out as fast as I could. I was expecting one of them, or a lot of them, to spring out of the darkness, but nothing happened.

Elizabeth popped out behind me and we made our way through the cellar, leaving the trapdoor open. Thanks to the light in the shaft, I could see a few feet in every direction, but the edges of the room were still cloaked in darkness.

I tapped Elizabeth's shoulder and pointed toward the corner where I thought the back door was located.

She nodded, and we crept around the boxes and paint cans that were strewn on the floor. Once we were a few feet away from the trapdoor, though, the light faded away. That's when I heard something. It was a shuffling sound. Someone *was* down here. They were walking.

Elizabeth reached for my shoulder. She was shaking, or maybe I was shaking, I couldn't tell. The footsteps were coming faster. Coming at us.

Maybe if I'd been able to keep my wits about me, I would have used the gun, but my wits were long gone. Instead, in an insane panic, I threw myself at the cellar doors, like a cartoon character rushing at a brick wall. And, like a terrified cartoon character, I actually managed to crash through them. Bashing through doors like that should have hurt, it should have hurt a lot, but apparently I'd managed to turn off the pain centers of my brain, and all without the help of a mysterious parasite.

Fresh air wafted across my face. The rain had let up and been replaced by a fine mist.

"Run!" Elizabeth screamed, rushing past me and into the backyard.

I spun around, holding the shotgun across my body, but Jimmy Brooks grabbed it and pulled me back down a few steps into the cellar. He yanked the gun out of my hands, tossed it sideways and snapped at me with a mouthful of needle-sharp fangs. I cringed, frozen, but an orange blur crossed in front of my face, and he fell backward into the cellar.

I looked up. Elizabeth was standing in the doorway. She'd kicked him square in the face.

"Run!" she screamed again, and I scrambled out of the cellar and across the lawn behind her.

The clouds were still blotting out the stars and the moon, but even in the dark, our orange unitards were going to make us stand out — unless we somehow managed to wander into a field full of prison inmates.

I skidded around the corner of the inn, but the padding on the feet of my unitard was soaked and slipping all around. I managed to catch my balance and glanced over my shoulder. Jimmy, Lennox and Baxter were rounding the corner behind me. I'd never make it to the car; I'd never be able to outrun them. I knew that for certain. But I could buy Elizabeth some time. She was almost at the front corner of the inn and might be able to make it into the woods if she had a few more seconds. Jake's pickup was parked in the driveway, beside the inn, leaving a gap that Elizabeth was just passing through now. If I fought them there, in that bottleneck, she might be able to get away.

Jimmy was close now; I could hear his footsteps pounding behind me as I reached the front bumper of Jake's truck. When I got to the passenger-side door, I tried to turn. My plan was to hit him with a surprise left hook, but my feet slipped sideways again and I fell, crashing into the side of the truck and landing on the gravel driveway.

Jimmy was running straight at me, his face expressionless, his mouth open. There was no way I could get back up in time. All I could do was watch in terror as he closed in on me, snapping his new fangs as he came. He was only a few feet away, when the passenger-side door flew open. I heard Jimmy thunk into it, face first, and then I watched him fall backward, Lennox and Baxter crashing into him and falling over him in a heap. I scrambled onto my feet, and Miles Van Helsing jumped out of the truck, holding a hammer in one hand and a wrench in the other.

"You're okay ..." I stammered.

"No time!" he said, shoving me toward the front of the inn.

By some miracle, the Porsche was parked in the driveway. I assumed the miracle went by the name of Miles Van Helsing. Elizabeth was getting into the driver's seat as we ran by Hal's precious rosebushes.

She slammed the door shut, and a moment later the car's engine roared to life. We only had about seven or eight feet to go when Dutton, the indestructible zompire, limped in front of us. His jaw was jutting off to the side, way out of place, and he could barely walk on one leg, but there he was, blocking our way.

Without a moment's hesitation, Miles threw the hammer at Dutton. It hit him right in the forehead. He wobbled backward, and Miles sprinted past him. Dutton blindly grabbed at me as I went by, but even in my soggy booties, I managed to scoot past him.

Miles was already in the backseat and had left the door open.

"Go!" I yelled, cramming myself in.

Elizabeth slammed on the gas, the tires spun and gravel spit out behind us. The car fishtailed before the tires caught, and Johnny's face slammed against my window. Dried blood covered his mouth and chin, and his nose was swollen and bent, probably thanks to Hal's smack with the gun. His lips were curled back, fangs snapping, but his eyes were empty.

I turned away. Did I really think I was going to get out of this? Maybe Hal had been right: it would have been better just to stay holed up in the bunker listening to old records.

"Go! Go! Go!" Miles cried, and the tires finally dug in. The car shot forward, and we tore out of the driveway. Johnny galloped along beside us, but I tried not to look; I didn't want to see him anymore, not like that.

"Hold tight," Elizabeth said, making a hard right onto Elm Street. She shifted gears, braked, shifted again, and all of a sudden we were speeding away.

Monday, 3:55 a.m.

We were hurtling down Elm Street, whipping around corners and practically catching air when we drove over the small rises in the road. It was still drizzling, so the visibility wasn't great, and the road was slick from the rain. None of it slowed Elizabeth down, though. I buckled up my seat belt and heard Miles doing the same behind me.

"I thought you were toast," I said, looking back at Miles.

"I thought you were, too."

"So what happened?" I asked.

"Your sister," Miles said. "One minute they were on top of me, the next she was dragging me across the cellar and then throwing me out the doors at the back."

"She's not infected! I knew she'd make it. That means Mom's probably still okay, too!" I said. "Where did she go?"

"I don't know," Miles said. "She just disappeared. I didn't stick around to investigate."

"Well, thanks for saving my neck, Miles," I said. "I figured you would've made a run for it instead of sticking around."

"I would have, but I ..." He hesitated. "I got turned around in the woods. By the time I made it back to Elm Street, the Porsche was gone. So, I backtracked to the inn and found it parked in the driveway."

"I bet it was Lilith," I said. "But why didn't you drive away?"

"Your brother and Dutton were patrolling the outside of the inn, and I couldn't get to the car. I slipped into Jake's truck and was waiting for a chance to make a break for the car, but they never left. That's bad, by the way," he added. "They're still capable of planning after sundown. It doesn't bode well."

"Well, what *does* bode well for us is that we can finally get out of this place. We can get help. Where are we headed?" I asked Elizabeth.

"We'll take Rolling River Road," Elizabeth said, "to Maple and try for the bridge. It'll only take fifteen minutes to get to Hillsboro once we're on the highway."

"As long as there are no roadblocks," Miles said. "The way they were rounding us up yesterday, I wouldn't be surprised if they tried to cordon off the town."

Before I could respond, Elizabeth made a hard left onto Rolling River Road. "Hold on!"

Just then, a leg fell over the side of the car.

I screamed, Miles screamed, Elizabeth screamed —

and then Johnny's face appeared in the windshield. He looked at us, upside down, for about two seconds, and then his face and leg disappeared again.

"Was that J-Johnny?" Miles stammered.

"Yeah," I groaned, then suddenly Johnny's face was next to me, at the passenger-side window.

I screamed again. So did Miles. Elizabeth leaned away from me, and the car swerved across the street. We hit the opposite shoulder and fishtailed. She pulled the wheel hard, too hard, back to the other side of the road. The car shot across the road and hit the gravel shoulder. Then Johnny was gone, and for a moment, it looked like we might have lost him. Elizabeth finally managed to get the car back under control, but then his face reappeared in the window beside me. He had the same wooden expression as before, like he couldn't care less about careening down the road on the roof of the car. He leaned even farther over the window. I saw his hand flash by and an instant later the window imploded. Tiny bits of glass rained down on me, and wind blasted in. Johnny leaned in and tried to bite me on the shoulder. I threw myself to the driver's side, away from him, crashing into Elizabeth's arms. The car jerked to the left and we swerved again. Elizabeth tried to straighten us up, but this time she couldn't. The car fishtailed wildly across the wet pavement, and for an instant, I recognized that we were back at The Bend. I even spotted the place where I'd jumped off the cliff. That was about when we hit the guardrail.

We plowed through it like a hot knife through butter,

hardly even slowing down. Then we were in the air.

As we hovered above the black water of the Rolling River, I heard Miles say "This is bad" in a ludicrously casual voice. Then we started our dive. The last thing I saw, before we hit the river, was the headlights lighting up the water. They penetrated the darkness until I thought I could see the very bottom.

Then, of course, we crash-landed. Johnny torpedoed off the roof and disappeared into the river. The car started to sink.

"Roll down your window, Elizabeth," Miles said calmly, as ice-cold water gushed into my window. "Roll it down before the electrical system fails."

She did, and water started gushing into her window, too.

"Make sure you unbuckle," Miles said, not quite as calmly as before. The frigid water was up to my waist now and pouring in fast. "Then take a deep breath and get out."

I unlocked my seat belt as the car tilted forward and started a nosedive. I took one last gasp of air before we were submerged. The car kept sinking for two or three more seconds before the front end hit the bottom. Then the headlights flickered out, and it got dark. My lungs were already screaming when I reached out for Elizabeth's arm, but I couldn't find her. I reached into the back, but Miles must have already evacuated, too. I pulled myself out of the car and kicked and clawed my way to the surface.

I burst out of the water, gasping and coughing.

"Elizabeth!" I yelled when I'd caught my breath. "Miles!"

The current of the river was stronger than I remembered, and it was quickly carrying me away from where the car had gone under.

"Elizabeth!"

"Over here!" she cried, and I spotted her orange jumpsuit downriver. She was standing waist-deep in the water near the riverbank.

She clambered out and into the trees while I swam over. I straggled onto the shore and followed her into the woods.

"Are you all right?" I asked. She was soaked and shivering.

"I think so," she said. The rain had picked up again; the sound of it slapping against the leaves of the trees was deafening. "What happened to Miles?"

"I don't know," I said.

"And Johnny?"

"I saw him go into the water. I don't know after that."

"Now what?" she asked, her teeth chattering.

"We should keep moving. Maybe try to get out of town on foot."

"I've got to get some dry clothes first or I'll freeze."

"I know they've got plenty of T-shirts at Romero's."

"No, I was thinking we'd head for the church. Reverend Takahashi collects used clothes for people in Haiti, and he's famous for leaving the doors unlocked. We could sneak in, get out of these stupid uniforms and then try to walk to the highway."

"It doesn't feel right taking clothes for people in Haiti, but if we get out of this alive, I'll donate a whole box of new stuff — heck, I'll send them ten boxes of new stuff. The faster we get out of here the better. Miles was right — if they don't have roadblocks set up now, they will for sure by the morning. I'm sorry I made us go back to the inn, Winehurst. We should've played it safe and just hightailed it out of town. Miles and Jimmy would still be ..."

"We all agreed to do it," she said, teeth chattering. "And it was the right thing, Charlie. Plus, Miles might be all right. He might be close by. Maybe we should wait for him?"

"Johnny might be close by, too," I said. "I think if Miles was here, he'd order us to keep moving."

"There's a walking trail — it's just through the trees," she said, pointing behind us. "And there's a bridge that will take us back to the road."

"Ladies first," I said, and we bumbled our way through the trees and onto a narrow walking path. I kept looking back as we walked, to check if we were being followed, but I didn't see anything or anyone.

"It's not far," Elizabeth said.

About a minute later, we came to a wooden bridge.

"I want to rip the feet off of these things," Elizabeth said, as we started toward the bridge. "It's like walking on a couple of slimy sponges."

"I guess the bomb shelter clothing designers didn't think people would be swimming in them much. That's just poor planning in my opinion."

Elizabeth stopped when we stepped onto the bridge and glanced up and down the river. "Do you see anything, Charlie?"

"I can barely see to the other side of the bridge, Winehurst," I said.

Just then I distinctly heard the cracking of branches. Someone was coming through the woods, and they weren't far away.

"Is it Miles?" Elizabeth asked, grabbing my arm. If she'd grabbed my arm like that yesterday, I would have been on cloud nine. Now I would have given anything for Johnny to be back to normal and stealing her away from me.

"I certainly hope so," I croaked, "but he would be the one person in the world who would completely understand if we didn't hang around to find out."

She nodded, and we dashed across the bridge. Once we popped out on the other side, we hustled down a winding gravel path and stopped behind a neighborhood mailbox.

"That's Maple," she whispered, nodding down the street. "It's not far to Church Street."

"How far?" I asked, keeping my ears peeled for anyone following us.

"Maybe five hundred yards?" she said.

I didn't like the fact that I couldn't hear anything behind us anymore. I would have absolutely hated it if I *could* hear someone coming, but not hearing anything was making me feel a whole new level of scared. On top of that, there was no good way to sneak along Maple Drive. The front yards were big and wide open, and you'd have to be blind to miss us with those orange jumpsuits.

"I think we're just going to have to run for it, Winehurst," I said.

"I'm probably going to break my ankle thanks to these booties," she said. Her skin was pale and she was shivering in violent bursts. "I can't wait to get into some new clothes."

"Yeah," I muttered, shivering, too, and scanned the street for the slightest bit of movement. But I didn't see a thing, which made me more terrified than ever. "Maybe we should try to sneak through the backyards."

"Maybe we ..." she started, and then we heard the thumps of footsteps coming across the bridge.

"On second thought, maybe we should just run," I said.

An instant later we were sprinting down Maple, my feet skidding left and right over the slick soles of the booties. Elizabeth stumbled a couple of times and lost some ground, but we managed to cover about four hundred yards pretty quickly. I could just see the church through the darkness when I slowed and glanced over my shoulder to make sure she was all right. That's when she tripped and fell onto the road in a heap. I stopped, slipping and almost falling, too, but I managed to catch my balance. Just as I started back, I caught sight of a figure walking onto Maple, emerging from the path we'd been on. And even though he was infected now, he still had his rock-star stroll, like he had nowhere to go and nothing important to do. Johnny.

Elizabeth scrambled onto her feet. "Run, Charlie!" she screamed.

"We're getting out of here together, Winehurst," I cried, rushing back and grabbing her hand. And with that, as if they'd just been waiting to prove me wrong, a slew of blank-faced zompires started emerging from the front doors along Maple Drive.

"Run!" Elizabeth said, squeezing my hand so tight I thought she might break a few bones.

We ran, stumbling, almost tripping, as twenty or thirty zompires came out of their houses and joined in the chase behind us. Lucky for us they seemed confused at first, like they couldn't figure out where we were, but within seconds, they started toward us with that eerie speed.

If they'd seen us any earlier, we never would have had a chance to make it to the church, but we'd already covered most of the distance, and now our terror was making us move with our own extra bit of speed. They were closing in fast, though, I could feel that without having to look. I don't know why I thought getting inside the church was going to make us safe, but it had to be better than being hunted down like a gazelle on the Serengeti.

My hopes were dashed almost immediately by another mob of about thirty zompires that marched off of Church Street, with jerky steps, and headed straight for the front of the church.

"This way!" Elizabeth cried, swerving to our right and sprinting toward the rear of the church.

"The back door," she panted. "He leaves it open."

A giddy panic set in, and I had to fight to keep myself from giggling as we made our mad dash for the back of the church. Zompires were right on top of us, and the new mob was already streaming around the front corner. It was pointless, I knew that, and yet we kept going. Then the back door came into view, and a foolish glimmer of hope spread through me. Maybe we could hide inside, lock ourselves in a room, wait it out? Maybe we could find a phone and call someone and they'd actually believe us and send help? Or maybe we'd find a time machine inside and travel back to three days ago? They were all ridiculous thoughts, but when Elizabeth got to the door and threw it open, I felt a gigantic wave of triumph crash over me. We bounded inside, and I slammed it shut. Elizabeth grabbed the dead bolt and twisted it into place.

"We might make it," I said. Then the mob crashed into the door, and I heard the wood crack.

"They're coming in!" Elizabeth groaned.

We were on a landing. There were stairs up, and there were stairs down.

"Which way?" I asked.

Elizabeth took the stairs up, and I followed her. We rushed along a short hallway, through a door, and found ourselves in the nave of the church. Elizabeth turned around and slammed that door shut, too, then scanned the room.

"Turn on the lights, Charlie," she said. "I can't stand the dark anymore. The switches are at the front."

I knew what she meant. If we were going down, and we almost certainly were, it would be nice to at least do it in the light. I rushed to the front and found a panel of about eight light switches. I used both hands and threw them all up at once. The lights blinked on, and the church got bright. At the same time, a recording of church bells started up. I froze momentarily, but reminded myself we weren't going to hide from them anymore, so church bells ringing didn't matter. Plus, if Miles, Lilith and Mom were out there somewhere, maybe it would create a diversion and give them a chance to escape.

I could hear footsteps rushing behind the door at the back. Elizabeth leaped away from it and dove under the pews. I dove, too, and we started commando crawling our way toward each other. The door crashed open, and I heard a crowd trample in.

There was no getting away now, and I knew it. The sad thing is I actually felt a wave of relief.

"It's been nice getting to know you, Winehurst," I whispered. "Maybe, after we're changed, we can still do dinner. And if we do share a hive mind, please ignore most of my thoughts. They can be pretty childish."

She grabbed my hands, smiled and gave me a short, simple kiss on the lips. "We tried," she said.

Feet closed in, all around us. I looked up from under the pew and saw the Man-Bear, Igor Balic, crouching down, looking right at me. His mouth was open, thorny teeth in full display, spider blossoms scampering across them.

Elizabeth squeezed my hands tighter. Balic started toward us, then hesitated and stood up. An instant later, the windows were crashing in. Something — no, lots of things — whistled through the air, and I looked at Elizabeth. She was staring at something — a green canister that was lying several feet away from her on the floor, hissing out yellow smoke. My eyes started to water, and I began to choke. I looked up at Balic again and saw a small dart shoot into his cheek, and then another hit him in the neck. My eyes felt like they were on fire and started watering so badly I couldn't see anymore. I didn't want to get up, but I needed to get away from the yellow smoke that was now billowing out of that canister. I staggered blindly to my feet, then I felt something sharp dig into my stomach. I looked down; a dart was sticking out of my orange jumpsuit. Everything went black.

Monday, ?:??

I woke up in a cot, in a white tent, with Richard O'Rourke staring down at me from behind a plastic visor. He was decked out in a yellow hazmat suit. I'd finally lost my mind.

"Hello, Harker," he said.

"Hola, O'Rourke, I think I've gone *loco*," I murmured.

"Yeah, sure, a long time ago. It probably happened after about a week at Choke."

"What? What's going on? I don't understand."

"You emailed me, remember?"

"I did?"

"Yeah, you said something strange was going on in Rolling Hills and sent me a photo of a skull with something growing out of it."

"Right," I mumbled. "How'd you get here so fast? I thought you were holed up somewhere in the Middle East."

"We're only three days into summer vacation, Harker. I haven't had time to pack, let alone leave."

"Where am I?"

"This is a containment tent, inside a mobile field hospital."

"In Rolling Hills?" I asked, looking around at the gleaming white walls of the tent.

"Close by," he said.

I tried to sit up, but the world went spinning away, and I collapsed back onto the bed.

"What happened?"

"Do you want the long or short version?"

"Medium?"

"All right," he said, sitting back. "Well, I got your email and, obviously, thought it was a joke. But I had to admit it seemed a little too elaborate for you, so I took some time to do some googling about Rolling Hills. There's someone by the name of Dr. Xavier Vortex, who's been tweeting and blogging about this mysterious viral outbreak about every five minutes, which is lucky for you. Otherwise, I wouldn't have risked telling my dad about it. But, after seeing that this Vortex had some serious credentials, scientifically speaking, I decided to broach the subject with him."

"Vortex actually has credentials?"

"Yes, he does — although he's kind of fallen off the map recently. Anyway, I brought it up with my dad, and he had one of his operatives come and check it out."

"What did he say?"

"Nothing. He never reported back. I don't think Dad would've handled things so ... well, so *efficiently*, if one of his own employees hadn't disappeared. That's not normal, and Dad takes his operatives' safety very seriously."

"This is all your dad?"

"His company, yes, and don't ask me who he's talked to or who he's working with on this. When he picks up the phone, I've been trained to stop listening. Look, I'm probably telling you more than I should, Harker, but we're friends, and I thought you should know something about what's going on."

"How'd you find us?"

"Dad and his team were actually in the middle of corralling the ... how does he put it? Oh yeah, he was corralling the 'contaminated subjects' on Church Street when he heard church bells and sent a squad of men over to investigate. He'd brought me along to ID you if you were ever captured, but he had me wait back here."

"What happened to the girl who was with me?"

"They're keeping you all separated until they're positive you're not infected. But from what I've heard, she's all right."

"Do you know what happened to Lilith or my mom?"

He frowned and shook his head. "They haven't brought them in yet, but my dad will let me know when they do. They've captured Johnny, though."

"What are they going to do with him? Can they cure him?"

"I don't know, Harker, but I will tell you this: Dad brought along some serious firepower on this job. They definitely have the best and brightest looking after him."

"So, what's in store for me?"

"For now, you can just sit back and relax. But I wouldn't start booking tee times anytime soon. The town is quarantined, and you may have been exposed to a seriously messed-up virus."

"Is that why you've got your rainsuit on?"

"It's called a hazmat suit, Harker. And I had to steal it to sneak in here. If anyone catches me, I might actually disappear for a few years — no joke."

"You'll let me know if they find my mom and Lilith, right?"

"Of course, but hey, you should know they brought in another guy a little while ago. He's in the room across the hall. He's hurt pretty bad, but I heard he mumbled your name a couple of times. I thought he might be a friend of yours."

"Is it Miles?" I asked.

He opened his mouth to answer, but then there was a rustling outside the tent followed by the sound of a zipper being undone. O'Rourke bolted up and stood at attention.

Two people entered, both decked out in hazmat suits.

O'Rourke saluted them and quickly marched out without another word.

One of my new visitors saluted him back, without really paying any attention, and walked over to me.

"Charles Harker, I'm Colonel Stephen H. Sanders. How the heck are you feeling, son?" he asked and bent over to peer at me. His face was clean-shaven and angular.

"I'm alive," I said. "I think."

"Damn straight you're alive," he said. "And you're a hero."

"Not me," I muttered. "I was running around like a chicken with my head cut off most of the time."

"There are worse things to be than a chicken," Sanders said. "Now buck up, son, because I've got some good news. Doc Peters here," he said, motioning to the other person, "has given you the all clear. You're not infected."

"Great," I said, even though being in the clear wasn't making me feel a whole lot better considering the rest of my family was either missing or infected.

"I'll get someone in here with some grub, and I'm sure you'll be feeling right as rain in no time. Now, if you'll excuse us, the doc's got rounds to make."

"Sure," I mumbled, but the two of them were already marching back to the zippered door. They unzipped, zipped and then were gone, leaving me alone in my quarantine tent.

"Miles Van Helsing," I muttered and sat up slowly. The world tilted a little again, but then things evened out. I eased my way onto my feet and expected to fall back down, but I got my balance. Whatever they'd put in that dart was wearing off.

"Miles Van Helsing," I said again, this time grinning a little. "That nut-ball made it."

I started toward the zipper-door, and that's when I clued in to the fact that I wasn't wearing my orange onesie anymore. Now I was decked out in a green hospital gown, the kind that's wide open in the back. I pulled it shut with one hand and grabbed the tent zipper.

I wanted to see Miles. We'd been through a heck of a lot, and I wanted to make sure he was okay.

I'd just managed to undo the zipper when someone burst in wearing one of those hazmat suits, practically knocking me over.

"Watch it," I said, figuring it was a doctor or a guard making sure I didn't go out for an unauthorized stroll. And I was going to head back to my bed like a good little patient when I caught sight of who was staring at me from behind the plastic visor.

"Miles!" I said and grabbed him.

"Take it easy," he said, as I tried to give him my version of a Johnny Harker bear hug.

"You made it!" I said, stepping back.

"You could say that," he said in a low voice. His face was covered in scrapes. One eye was swollen purple and completely shut. The other was only partially open.

"What happened?" I asked.

"The crash in the river," he said, zipping the tent closed. "Then I met your brother in the woods."

"How'd you get away?" I asked.

"I didn't," he said flatly.

"What —" I started, feeling my legs turning to rubber.

"I borrowed the suit from your friend," he said.

"O'Rourke?" I gasped and fell backward into my cot.

"He's in my room ... taking my place, temporarily. The suit will shield me from the sun."

"Not you, Miles ..." I said, and all my strength drained out of me.

"It needs to survive. It needs to move on. I have to get out of here or they'll try to kill it."

"Miles, they can fix you," I stammered.

"Fix me?" he said flatly and pulled a scalpel from out of nowhere. "I don't want to be fixed."

"Easy does it, Miles," I said, trying to gather up some energy to fight him off.

"This isn't for you," he said and stepped over to the other side of the tent. He sliced the scalpel down the side of the tent, and there was a sound like air seeping out. Then my tent sagged a little as sunlight streamed in from outside.

"I came to tell you, Charlie, that I have to go, but I'll be back," he said, taking one step outside. "Lilith and your mother, they're not one of us. Not yet. But you'll all join us, and you'll see that it's better this way."

"Miles!" I cried, but he was gone.

Also by James Leck

Meet Jack Lime, a self-styled P.I. who "solves problems" for his fellow students. In these cases, Jack navigates an underworld that teems with pimply gangstas and gum snapping femmes fatales — a.k.a. high school. Whether he's hunting hot bikes or rescuing hostage hamsters, no case is too small for this hard-boiled hero.

The Adventures of Jack Lime

PB 978-1-55453-365-7
ePub 978-1-77138-067-6

Booklist Top Ten First Novels for Youth

★ "You don't need to reinvent the wheel for a great detective story, but you do need a terrific sense of style. Jack Lime's got it in spades."

— *Booklist,* starred review

"With its tongue-in-cheek Raymond Chandler-esque first-person narration laced with gleefully clichéd slang, this one is perfect for Chet Gecko grads."

— *Kirkus Reviews*

The Further Adventures of Jack Lime

HCJ 978-1-55453-740-2
ePub 978-1-77138-068-3

Bank Street Best Books of the Year for Children and Young Adults

John Spray Mystery Award, Shortlist

"A winning formula, replete with wince-worthy contretemps reported in properly poker-faced prose."

— *Kirkus Reviews*

"An entertaining page-turner."

— *Canadian Children's Book News*